Casting Shadows

by

Margaret Tessler

ISBN 978-1-62141-844-3

Printed in the United States of America.

BookLocker.com, Inc.
2012

First Edition

AUTHOR'S NOTE

Many elements of this story are true. The beautiful Lodge Resort and Spa in Cloudcroft is real, and it does offer delightful mystery-theater weekends.

The story itself is a product of my own vivid imagination. I hope you'll get so caught up in it that you'll believe every word. However if you come across anything that doesn't jibe with actual facts, please overlook it and simply enjoy the ride.

For Howard
with love

ACKNOWLEDGMENTS

I am deeply indebted to the following people for their expertise in various fields, their advice and feedback, and their encouragement:

Russ Alberti; David Bachelor, Damon Fay; my sister, Louise Gibson; Nick Gonzales; Doug Lyle; Michael McGuire; my granddaughter Elliana Moran; my daughter Linda Moran; Tom and Marless Owen; Mike Schaller; my daughter-in-law Beth Tessler; my husband, Howard Tessler; and of course the members of my writing group: Mary Blanchard, Charlene Dietz, Edith Flaherty, Diane Flaherty, Jeanne Knight, Betsy Lackmann, Marcia Landau, Jan McConaghy, Helen Pilz, Joan Taitte, Pat Wood, and Mary Zerbe

I am especially grateful to my step-daughter Diane Tessler and to Lisa Thomassie for guiding me through The Lodge with their blessing.

As always, I take responsibility for the times I've strayed from their collective expertise and wisdom and wandered off on my own merry whim. They understand that I am, after all, a writer of fiction.

RECURRING CHARACTERS

Sharon & Ryan Salazar, whose vacation plans once again take an unexpected turn

Cat & Steve Córdova: Good friends who join the Salazars on their vacation; Sharon's former classmates

Alvina Piffle: Cat's disagreeable aunt

"Mr. Stetson" and "Mr. Nondescript": Patrons at café who get into discussion about online predators.

Keziah Porter: Missing 14-year-old
Jemma Porter: Keziah's older sister

Sheriff Gibson, Detective Sgt. Tom Alderete, and Deputy Roy Hendrix: Authorities in charge of investigation

Detective Sgt. Tom Alderete: Friend of Keziah and Jemma
Cindy Alderete: Tom's sister; Jemma's friend

Brenda and Darryl Taylor: Interfaith Teen Center volunteers who befriended Keziah. Mrs. Prettypenny and Sir Lostalot, respectively, in mystery play

Dot, Wilma, & Phyllis: Friends of Keziah
Joel: Classmate of Keziah

WINTER 2003
CHAPTER 1

You've heard of people—maybe even known a few—who don't have a mean bone in their bodies. Well, evidently all the leftover mean bones found their way into Alvina Piffle's body. And Alvina Piffle found her way into my life with a little help from my friend Cat Córdova.

"She's my aunt, my mother's youngest sister, and she signed up for the same Mystery Theater shindig we're going to," Cat had told me over the phone, her voice flat. "She's very independent, so she won't be hanging out with us, but my mom would feel better if we, uh, kind of kept an eye on her."

Since Cat was kind and generous by nature, I wondered why she sounded so unenthusiastic about honoring such a simple request. Maybe she felt it would interfere with our plans.

"It won't be any trouble at all," I reassured her. "In fact, she'd be welcome to join us anytime."

"Can you see me rolling my eyes through the telephone lines?"

"Can you see me brushing away all our worries with a wave of my hand?"

We laughed and ended our call. Nothing could dim my excitement over our upcoming pre-Christmas holiday.

My name is Sharon Salazar. My husband, Ryan, and I live in San Antonio, Texas, where he's a high-school Spanish teacher and I'm a lawyer. Whenever we take a few days off from work, if we go with anyone else at all, it's usually with some of our relatives. I say "our" relatives, even though—strictly speaking—there are only three on "my side" and about 200 on Ryan's.

However, this time our friends the Córdovas, Cat and Steve, were joining us on a trip to Cloudcroft, New Mexico, to take part in an interactive mystery play.

Afterwards, the Córdovas would head back to San Antonio while Ryan and I would stay another week or two in Cloudcroft. Ryan had a long winter break, and I'd been asked to participate in a legal symposium—a way of combining business with pleasure.

The first few days of December zipped by, and I never gave Cat's Aunt Alvina another thought. I'd barely had time to finish writing cards and wrapping presents when it was time to leave.

The Córdovas met us at the airport, where we all boarded an early-morning flight to El Paso. Once we arrived, we rented a van large enough to accommodate suitcases stuffed with heavy winter gear, as well as the cross-country ski equipment we planned to rent.

It was 70 degrees all the way from El Paso to Alamogordo, but we soon left the warmth of the desert as we climbed toward the mountains surrounding Cloudcroft, about sixteen steep miles away. Ponderosa pines with a light dusting of snow greeted us along the winding highway into town.

We had reservations at The Lodge, an impressive Old-World-style building atop a hill. The inn's three stories were crowned with a lookout tower, rumored to be visited at times by mysterious apparitions—most often the ghost of the beautiful red-haired Rebecca.

As we drove onto the circular driveway in front, I noticed a figure huddled on a nearby wrought-iron bench and bundled in so many coats and blankets, he—or she—looked a little like the abominable snowman. The only sign of life was the glowing red tip of a cigarette that protruded from a slit in the wooly gray scarf covering its face.

We'd no sooner checked in than the snowman, sans scarf and cigarette, accosted Cat, whose ashen face revealed her dismay.

"Aunt Alvina, I didn't expect you till tomorrow."

CHAPTER 2

"I didn't expect you today either," Alvina said. The woman had white hair, blunt-cut just below her ears, icy blue eyes, and a fearsome scowl. "Almost didn't recognize you, Caterina. Looks like you've put on a few pounds."

"Only where it counts," Steve said. He set down their suitcases, put his arm around Cat, and gave her shoulder a gentle squeeze.

"Who asked you?" Alvina retorted.

Ryan and I glanced at each other, not sure if we should edge away and leave the Córdovas to fend for themselves or stay and wait it out.

"All for one," Ryan whispered, setting down our own suitcases.

"God, it's hot in here." Alvina turned toward the back of the lobby, where a cheerful blaze was glowing in the fireplace. "Why do they have that stinky fire going?"

"I'm sure it'll be pleasant once we take off our coats," Cat said. "We're on our way to our rooms now."

"I'd go to mine too, but there's nowhere to smoke in this damn place. A person can't even be comfortable in their own room."

Cat smiled. "I'm sorry. I guess we'll have to make do. So...we'll be on our way now."

"Not so fast, missy." Alvina jerked her head toward us. "Who are these people?"

"I'm sorry," Cat said again, her voice contrite. "I didn't mean to be in such a hurry."

Cat introduced us; Ryan and I murmured appropriate responses. I tried to smile, but must not have been too convincing.

Alvina glared at me in return. "What are you staring at?"

"I'm sorry. I didn't realize...."

It occurred to me that there were a lot of "I'm sorrys" going around to the person who least deserved them.

"'I didn't realize,'" she mimicked. "You should pay attention."

Actually, I HAD *been staring. Trying to see even one smidgen of resemblance between you and Cat.*

"It's been a hectic morning, Aunt Alvina," Cat said. "I'm sure we're all a little bleary-eyed. We'll catch up with you later."

Then, before Alvina could waylay us further, the four of us excused ourselves, leaving her to direct her complaints to the management. In the background, we could hear her berating the desk clerk about the accommodations, the service, the heat inside, the cold outside, and numerous other infractions for which she held the inn responsible.

*   *   *

Our spirits picked up once we were out of earshot. We were delighted to find our rooms cozy and charming. Naturally, Cat and I had to check out each other's rooms, both of which shared a Victorian motif, with a patterned quilt on each bed, ruffled pillow shams, and brocade drapes and valences. Oak furniture and tiffany lamps added to the ambiance. Paisley teddy bears made themselves at home on plush armchairs. Yet each room had is own distinct flavor. The Córdovas' was decorated in shades of blue and peach, ours in various greens, with splashes of burgundy.

After our inspection, Steve and Ryan reminded us that we hadn't eaten anything but peanuts since breakfast. We planned to have dinner at the Lodge, so thought it would be fun to have lunch someplace in town. We headed toward the lobby to ask about good places to try.

"Wait," Cat said as we reached the intersection where our hallway joined the main hallway. "Let's make sure the coast is clear." We sneaked down the hall, pressed close to the walls, listening for sounds of Alvina's sniping.

Hearing nothing but the happy chattering of other guests, we stepped up to the desk with our questions.

The clerk, whose nametag read "Laura," was polite but cool. She suggested a few places to eat, then cleared her throat and asked, "Aren't you here with Ms. Piffle?"

Cat's cheeks turned red. "No. We're all here for the Mystery Weekend. Beyond that, we're each going our own way."

Laura's demeanor softened. "Pardon me for asking, but we were hoping, since you seem to know each other, that you could, ah...."

"Believe me, I would if I could."

"I shouldn't have said anything," Laura apologized. "It's not your problem. Just enjoy your lunch!"

* * *

We checked for Alvina outside the lodge, before picking up our pace.

"I can't believe we let that little old woman intimidate us," Steve grumbled as we hurried down the steps toward the parking lot. "Here we are—every darn one of us nearly forty years old—skulking through the hotel like schoolkids playing hooky."

We burst out laughing, imagining big burly Steve shaking in his boots. Ryan didn't fit the picture either. Not as tall or husky as Steve, he was still well built—certainly looked like someone who could hold his own against the likes of Alvina Piffle. Cat suggested I use my Karate skills to take Alvina down, creating a mental image that seemed even more comical.

Of course it would be a lot easier if physical prowess was all it took to stop Alvina's nastiness. But, besides not being inclined to fisticuffs, Cat and I weren't even scary looking. I was a hazel-eyed blonde with short curly hair. Cat always described herself as medium: Medium height, medium brown hair and eyes. In reality, she was quite pretty.

On the short ride into town, we mulled over Laura's suggestions and decided to have lunch at Ernie's Hot Dogs and Burgers. We placed our order at the counter, then moved into the dining area, which was large enough for only four tables and a booth. We chose the booth, situated against one wall.

Only two other tables were occupied. Seated at the table against the opposite wall was a tall, lanky, cowboy-type guy wearing a Western shirt, Levis, boots, and a Stetson. A rather nondescript man sat at the table between us, facing the cowboy but with his back to us.

Our burgers arrived, and we found ourselves too involved with our own meal and conversation to pay much attention to the other diners. Then, during a lull when we were doing more eating than talking, the cowboy turned to the other customer and said in a conversational tone:

"My wife got online last night and looked up registered sex offenders in our area. She showed me a picture of someone looked exactly like you."

If there had been a lull before, it was dead quiet now. I remembered to close my mouth before glancing over at the two men.

"Well, that certainly is a coincidence," Mr. Nondescript said in a monotone.

"Yessir, just like you," Mr. Stetson continued. "From somewhere up in Idaho. Where you from?"

"California."

"What brings you here?"

"Just passing through...on my way to Dallas."

"Big city like that. Easy to get lost."

I figured Mr. Nondescript would get up any minute now and walk away; then I could get a look at his face. But he just sat there as if he and Mr. Stetson were talking about the weather.

And the four of us just sat there like pillars of salt. I'd lost my appetite, but that didn't have anything to do with my hamburger turning cold.

Ryan cleared his throat. "Ready to go?"

We came out of our trance, but before we could even put on our coats, we were jarred by the sound of someone stomping into the café.

"Mind if I join you?" Alvina rasped, sliding into the booth beside Cat.

"How did you find us?" Cat blurted out. "I mean, sure, but we were just leaving."

So was Mr. Stetson. Ryan read my mind (a sometimes wonderful habit of his), and we rose to pay our bill while the Córdovas dealt with Alvina. This wasn't one of those fancy places where the waitress refills your coffee—or pays any attention to you at all. So Ryan and I met up with Mr. Stetson at the cash register.

On the way to the counter, I couldn't help but take a surreptitious look at Mr. Nondescript, who looked a little queasy. No wonder. He seemed rooted to his chair. I guess he wanted to make sure the cowboy had left before encountering him at the register.

By now, the Córdovas had disentangled themselves from Alvina and joined us in line. While taking care of our bills, we heard some kind of commotion coming from the dining area.

"Alvina!" Cat said. "I bet she stood in the doorway and overheard that bizarre conversation before she barged in on us. And now—"

And now there was silence. Cat peeked into the dining room, but no one was there. Instead, Alvina was waiting for us outside.

"He just ignored me and walked away," she growled. "Thinks he can get away with being a menace to society."

And apparently—in his haste to escape the wrath of Alvina—thinks he can leave without paying for his lunch either.

CHAPTER 3

Alvina still hadn't gotten around to eating her own lunch, so she went back to Ernie's while the rest of us left to rent ski equipment, a task she informed us would—good news!—bore her to death.

We walked to the rental place, a block away, where we learned about several good trails to take. We didn't talk about the strange events at Ernie's till we were back in the van. By then we were all fairly bursting with opinions and theories.

"The poor guy really looked stricken," I said while we all buckled up. "Maybe he's guilty—but maybe not. Maybe he was just embarrassed."

"I vote for shell-shocked," Cat said, looking over her shoulder from the front seat. "My guess is, he thought the cowboy was crazy—or looking for a fight or something."

I nodded. "And the guy didn't want to agitate him by arguing."

"You know what I think?" Steve said, as he maneuvered the van out of the parking lot and onto the main street. "I think both those guys were actors rehearsing their lines for the mystery play."

"No way," Cat said, laughing. "Who would write dialogue that bad?"

"I agree,'" Ryan put in. "It was too weird for anyone to make it up."

"If they *were* acting, they were really good," I added. "I guess we'll find out tonight when we see the Mystery Theater in action."

* * *

I've always found cross-country skiing both soothing and exhilarating. A powdery snow had fallen early that morning, and someone else had broken trail before us, so we soon found ourselves gliding among the evergreens, with sunny blue skies above.

After a while, Cat stopped and took a few moments to breathe in the crisp fragrant air. "I do believe this is heaven!"

I pulled up beside her. "In that case, we need to make snow angels."

Within seconds, we'd all taken off our skis to lie side by side in the snow and fashion our "angel wings." Then we stood up to inspect our handiwork.

"Beautiful," Cat said, brushing the snow off her parka. "Looks a little like those paper cut-out things we used to make in kindergarten. On a much larger scale of course."

We decided this was a good way to end the excursion, go back to the Lodge, and rest up before the dinner theater tonight.

"Good timing," Ryan said. "Looks like the sun has quit for the day."

The sky had gradually changed to the kind of dull misty white that promises more snow. We attached our skis again and headed back toward the van, parked in a turnoff at the trailhead. The trail was narrow, so we skied single-file.

Cat, taking her turn at the lead, swerved unexpectedly into a wide opening in the path and motioned for us to follow.

"It looks like someone might have fallen," she said. "Behind that small piñon across the road. I guess we wouldn't have seen anything on the way up."

Steve pulled up behind her and adjusted his snow goggles. "Just looks like a coat to me. Someone probably dressed in layers. Peeled it off when it got too warm. Figured they'd come back for it later."

A coat—if that's what it was—barely visible under a thin layer of snow.

"It hasn't snowed in several hours," I said. "If it's a jacket or whatever, seems like someone would have come back for it by now."

"And whoever broke trail is long gone," Cat added. "We haven't seen anyone else, coming or going."

We all looked at one another, uneasiness creeping over us like the sudden chill in the air.

"We'd better check it out. Wait here," Ryan said, as he and Steve skied toward the object.

Cat and I ignored Ryan's warning and followed till we were all standing together on ground made uneven and lumpy by fallen pine cones and underbrush. Steve was partly right. From a distance, a coat was all that could be seen. But up close we could see the form of a person huddled under the snow.

My stomach did a somersault. Cat's eyes widened as she struggled for breath. We all must have looked as pale as the sky overhead.

Ryan sidestepped closer, knelt, and tried unsuccessfully to brush the snow aside. "Hardened into ice crystals now. Whoever it is has been here awhile—probably all night."

Maybe longer. How long does a person stay mummified in ice?

I forced myself to look again. The body was lying on its side, knees bent, arms folded across its stomach, as if trying to hold in warmth. Fully dressed in a bulky red parka and hood, white ski pants, and mittens. The face, which had a purplish hue, was partly obscured by a long scarf. Young, old, male, female—impossible to tell. There was something almost grotesque about the anonymity.

With trembling fingers, I shed my gloves and dug my cell phone out of my pocket. "I have a signal. Not too strong. I'll call 911."

* * *

While waiting for the authorities to arrive, we skied back to the trail we'd just left, then continued several feet in both directions, partly to keep warm and partly just for something to do. We didn't want to leave the area, but also didn't want to lose sight of each other.

"What was this person doing here?" I murmured, looking up and down the trail and thinking out loud. "I haven't seen any skis, or poles, or snowshoes—or anything like that. They couldn't have been *completely* covered with snow. Besides, it isn't even that deep."

"A hiker maybe?" Steve said. "I suppose if there were any footprints, we've pretty well skied over them by now."

"Could be a hiker," Ryan said. "But it's still odd. If he was alone, seems like he'd have stuck to the trail."

Cat shuddered. "And if he—or she—wasn't alone...."

While we were puzzling, three men from the sheriff's department and someone from the medical examiner's office arrived, having taken advantage of a forest service road that paralleled the ski trail. They trudged toward us in their sturdy boots and introduced themselves.

They ranged in height from Sheriff Gibson at the short end to Deputy Hendrix, who appeared to be about six-foot-four. In between were the M.E. and Detective Sergeant Alderete. Otherwise, it was hard to distinguish them since they all wore dark glasses against the snow's glare and fur trapper hats. Bundled up against the cold, the men seemed quite hefty.

Sgt. Alderete took us aside to get our names and statements while the others approached the frigid body, careful to avoid our ski tracks and watch where they made their own bootprints.

"How did you happen to find the body?" the detective asked us after jotting down the initial information.

"We didn't know...we th-thought...." Cat's teeth started chattering.

Steve side-stepped closer to Cat and gave her a hug. "My wife spotted it first. The red coat caught her eye."

The detective's fingers tightened their grip on his Bic pen.

"She thought someone might have fallen," Steve continued. "So we came over to find out."

Sgt. Alderete surveyed the area and frowned. "Did you move the body? Turn it over?"

"No," I said. "I'm sorry for the tracks and everything." *If this turns out to be a crime scene, we've definitely contaminated it.* "We just didn't realize what we were getting into. I mean, I know it seems obvious now, but when we first got here, we didn't know the—the person—was already—" I closed my eyes, mentally taking in the scene again.

"I guess we hoped we could rescue someone," Ryan said.

"Hey, Tom," Deputy Hendrix called out, hoisting his camera over his shoulder. "Looks like we found Keziah Porter."

Sgt. Tom Alderete clenched his jaw and turned away.

"Slow down, Roy," the sheriff said sharply.

I glanced up to see him nodding toward us but scowling at Deputy Roy Hendrix.

Sgt. Alderete snapped his notebook shut. "That should do it for now," he told us. "No sense you guys standing out here in the cold."

Sheriff Gibson and the other two men crunched through the snow to where we were standing.

"Got everything you need, Tom?" the sheriff asked.

"Yes, sir. These folks are here on vacation. Staying at the lodge to see that play. They'll be here a few more days."

"Good." The sheriff turned to us. "We'll call you if we need to." A few snowflakes began falling, and he took out a large handkerchief to wipe off his glasses. Lines around his brown eyes made him appear older than I'd originally thought. Mid-fiftyish? Sadder too.

Then he smiled, lightening the weariness he seemed to feel. "My sister's in the play. She's 'Mrs. Feelbad.' I hope it'll help take your minds off...." He shook his head and put his glasses back on, then waved us on our way. "Stay warm."

CHAPTER 4

The van was parked less than half a mile away, and the sheer physical motion of skiing toward it helped clear our minds, even though the rhythm seemed mechanical rather than pleasurable this time. None of us had much to say on the ride back, absorbed in our own thoughts, or maybe just not up to rehashing the somber ending to our excursion. Ryan offered to return the rental equipment, then dropped the rest of us off at the lodge.

"I'd like a glass of wine," Cat said softly, as if she still couldn't trust her voice. "Join us, Sharon?"

I shook my head. "Thanks. Maybe later."

The truth was, I found the cheerfulness of the lobby jarring, so wanted nothing more than to go straight to our room. There I shed my ski clothes, undressing as if in slow motion.

The show must go on. But I was thankful that dinner was still two hours away. After showering, I wrapped myself in my terry-cloth robe, the pale aqua robe that used to be turquoise.

I'd hesitated about including it with the new clothes I'd packed for the occasion. But, worn and faded though it was, it was like an old friend, and I was glad I'd brought it along. I sat in the roomy armchair with the teddy bear in my lap, hoping to decompress, but my mind wouldn't let go.

Deputy Hendrix's words echoed in my mind: *Looks like we found Keziah Porter*. Found. How long had she been lost—or missing? Who was she? I hoped her death was accidental, but even that raised questions.

Where was Ryan? Probably with the Córdovas. I should get dressed.... I should....

Ryan's touch on my arm was light, but I sat up with a jolt. *Where am I? How long have I been asleep?* I rubbed my eyes. "What time is it?"

"A little after 5:00." He leaned down and kissed the top of my head. "You smell good even if your hair is crooked."

I wrinkled my nose at him. "Thanks." My hair had dried at odd angles, springing out of my head like electric coils. Nothing a little—or maybe a lot of—mousse couldn't cure. I stood and yawned. "5:00 already? Guess we'd better get ready for dinner."

"You're right. I'll go hop in the shower."

Before disappearing into the bathroom, he handed me a somewhat wrinkled 5" x 7" flyer. "Here, take a look at this."

I smoothed the flyer out and began reading. The hand-printed heading read, "HAVE YOU SEEN ME?" Underneath was a grainy black-and-white photo of a girl who looked to be about fourteen or so. Underneath that was the name "KEZIAH PORTER." This was followed by one stark statement about her disappearance: "Last seen in Alamogordo on November 16."

November 16—that was just a few weeks ago! I couldn't believe she'd been on the mountain all this time. I marched into the bathroom, shaking the flyer and shouting at Ryan above the noise of the running water. "Where did you get this?"

"I'll tell you all about it in a minute," he shouted back.

"Well, make it a fast minute."

Back in the bedroom, I sat in the easy chair again and waited impatiently for the sound of the water to be turned off, the shower curtain wrenched back. I studied the flyer again and noticed pinpricks in each of the four corners. I supposed it had been thumbtacked somewhere around town and wondered if there were more flyers that we'd somehow overlooked.

I also wondered how old Keziah was when the picture was taken and how old she was now. No details were given about the color of her eyes or hair, but she appeared to be Anglo. Her hair was pulled back from her face. In a pony tail? Too bad I couldn't see the back of her head. Her face was sweet, yet somewhat vapid. Well, it wasn't fair to judge by one photo.

Ryan finally emerged from the shower, one towel around his middle, another draped around his shoulders.

I jumped up from the chair. "Tell me!"

"Just a cotton-pickin' minute. Let me get some clothes on."

"*Another* minute? You've had two already."

He grinned and began dressing in a way that seemed deliberately leisurely to me.

Two could play this game. I faced the mirror on the dresser and turned my attention to my unruly hair.

"Cat's aunt gave me the flyer," Ryan said as tucked his shirttail into his slacks. "Rather, she threw it at me."

"Oh, my." I turned toward Ryan again as my mind began racing with a hundred semi-connected questions. "Why? Does Aunt Alvina know anything about...this afternoon? Cat didn't tell her, did she? Besides, we're not absolutely sure who we found. Maybe Deputy Hendrix simply jumped to the wrong conclusion...knowing Keziah Porter was missing—"

"Hold on. Lots of wrong-conclusion-jumping around here. Alvina found the flyer tacked up in a convenience store and is convinced Keziah's disappearance has something to do with that conversation we heard at lunch."

"So why did she take it down and foist it off on you?"

Ryan sat in the easy chair I'd vacated to put on his socks and shoes. "Well, she foisted it off on Cat and Steve first. I went to look for them in the bar and found out Alvina had already cornered them."

"Do you think she was fishing for information?"

"Nah. I think she was just off on her own agenda."

"Did anyone suggest she go to the sheriff with her...suspicions?"

Ryan shook his head. "What happened, Steve went along with her. Told her she was probably right and asked her how she planned to find the guy. She yelled at Steve that she didn't need his sarcasm."

"Poor Steve."

Ryan leaned back in the chair. "I asked Steve if I could see the flyer. That's when Alvina snatched it from him and flung it at me."

"What 'sarcastic' suggestion did *you* make?"

"I said, 'Hmm.' Quote, unquote. She said we were all a bunch of morons and stomped off. I think we were all a little shook, to tell you the truth. It hit closer to home than we would have admitted to that old bat."

I nodded. "It is unsettling." I looked at the flyer again. "If the girl we found really is Keziah Porter, I wonder what happened to her...and how she wound up on that mountain."

CHAPTER 5

We met up with the Córdovas in the lobby, hoping that Aunt Alvina wouldn't want to associate with a bunch of morons. Luck was with us.

Several of us watched in awe as staff members completed decorating a magnificent Christmas tree—a fragrant Douglas fir. A hydraulic ladder carried staffers up to trim the highest branches since the ceiling rose nearly two stories. As a finishing touch, someone placed a handcrafted silver star at the very top. We oohed and aahed and applauded as the ladder was moved away so we could admire the colorful lights and ornaments.

Luck ran out about then. We heard Alvina clomp into the lobby, complaining that trees—all varieties apparently—gave her a headache, and she hoped there wasn't one where the event was to take place. I hoped there *was* one so we could sit next to it and she wouldn't want to join us.

She scowled at Cat and me. "Why are you dressed like that? That your idea of 'casual'?"

"Well, yes," Cat answered evenly. She was wearing a burgundy-colored dress with a scoop neckline, and a single strand of pearls.

"Mine too." I'd worn a forest-green velour pantsuit with a softly draping cowl neck. One of my favorite selections from my favorite Goodwill outlet.

"You look nice, Aunt Alvina," Cat told her.

I nodded, searching my brain for something complimentary to say about Alvina's unadorned sweater and slacks. *Gray is your color* was all that came to mind, so I kept my mouth shut.

By then it was time for dinner to start. Alvina tromped upstairs ahead of us, so we hung back long enough for other guests to file in between us.

We met in one of the smaller ballrooms. The setup was ideal, with a stage at one end of the room and the buffet table at the far end. A small bar lined the wall facing the windows that looked out on the snowy landscape. In the middle of the room were round tables large enough to seat six to eight people.

Alvina was one of the first in line at the buffet table, and even from a safe distance, we could hear her griping about the wide array of food. "Can't stand shrimp. Makes me break out in hives just being in the same room.... Cantaloupe? Ugh! What idiot suggested that? Makes my throat close up. Pineapple too...."

To counteract her criticism, we found ourselves fairly gushing over the lavish spread. We lingered over our choices until we could see where Alvina settled, then found seats at the opposite side of the room.

"In case you haven't noticed," Cat remarked, "Aunt Alvina's allergies are very selective. In other words, she's only allergic to whatever other people love."

We laughed and began chatting amiably. Another couple joined us, but we'd barely exchanged names when Alvina marched over. She plunked her plate down between Cat and Steve, hauled an empty chair to our table, and sat down. The other couple made polite excuses and made their getaway.

"Are you enjoying yourself, Aunt Alvina?" Cat asked sweetly.

"Woman sitting next to me at that other table—too damn much perfume."

"That's too bad. They looked like friendly people," Cat replied.

"All they could talk about was their stupid cats. Cats give me hay fever. My whole head swells up."

"We have a cat," I said.

Alvina's eyes narrowed. "You didn't bring it with you, did you?"

"No, he's with our nephew right now."

An idea struck me. "I know how you feel. Cat fur all over the place. It's always on my clothes. Just can't get rid of it no matter how hard I try."

But the notion that I might be covered from head to toe with cat hair didn't faze Alvina. And I couldn't help noticing that her plate was filled with a number of tasty-looking items, so she must have overlooked some of her food allergies as well. She ate heartily, grumbling the whole time.

We tuned her out and carried on our own conversation as we finished our meal. Before long, it was time for the play to begin.

Despite the events of the day, I found myself fully involved in *Murder Most Dastardly*, the satirical mystery that unfolded. The actors said their lines with mock seriousness, deliberately out of sync with their sweeping melodramatic gestures. The villainous Snaky Swindlesall made enough enemies that suspects ran rampant after he was conveniently dispatched with strychnine-laced prune juice.

The production itself lasted only thirty minutes, followed by an hour or so during which the actors mingled with the audience. It reminded me of an open house, with people standing in groups scattered around the room or at the bar.

Surprisingly, Alvina must have been absorbed in the play also, since she busied herself collaring various actors instead of trailing us. At least I *supposed* she was garnering clues to the fake murder, since—another first—her voice wasn't carrying above the crowd.

I was curious to speak with Sheriff Gibson's sister Louise, who, as Mrs. Feelbad, seemed to lead the fray of suspects. I latched onto her as soon as a couple of people ahead of me moved on to other actors.

I asked a few questions about her role, while she gave answers that were either true or meant to mislead (since that was part of the game).

"I'd like to talk to you before you leave, if you have a few minutes," I said.

She raised her eyebrows. "About the play?"

"No." I hesitated. "About Keziah Porter."

She stiffened. "Idle curiosity?"

"No...." I started to explain, but she cut me off.

"You're the second person to ask me about her."

"Oh?" I wondered if it was Alvina who'd gotten there before me. I hadn't paid attention to the actors she was presumably interviewing.

Just then another guest zoomed over to take a turn questioning Mrs. Feelbad.

"I'm sorry for bringing this up at a bad time," I said. "Maybe we can talk later."

"We'll see," she said noncommittally before turning to the newcomer.

I scanned the room for Alvina. I wanted to find out exactly how she was "interrogating" people, if that was the case, hoping she hadn't alienated anyone else. I was about to catch up with her when another actor laid his hand on my arm. "Sir Lostalot."

"I overheard you ask Louise about Keziah Porter."

Hmm. He hadn't even bothered to stay in character. Still, his poker face reminded me that he was indeed a good actor. Did he think I was out of line? Maybe Alvina wasn't the only one to offend people.

"I'm afraid it was bad timing on my part. I was concerned when I saw the flyers and couldn't help wondering about her. The whole town must have been affected by her disappearance."

A trace of worry appeared in his brown eyes. When he brushed his wispy hair off his forehead, I realized he was wearing a wig and was probably younger than the downtrodden loser he played. Probably smarter too.

"People were shocked, of course. But it's been several weeks now, and I was beginning to think no one even looked at those faded flyers anymore."

Another guest stepped up beside us, a look of patience in her face and one of impatience in the tap of her foot.

"Don't go away." Sir Lostalot said to me before smiling at the other guest.

"I'll be back," I said, then continued my quest for Alvina. She was nowhere in sight. What was she up to now?

CHAPTER 6

Instead of finding Alvina, I caught up with Ryan, and we compared notes on our respective conversations with the "suspects." Ryan thought he'd picked up some clues, but I had to admit I'd been too distracted.

Cat and Steve joined us and added their observations, which led to a lively discussion, since none of us agreed on the conclusions we'd reached.

"Have you seen Alvina lately?" I asked.

"She said something about chasing ghosts and went her own way," Cat said.

Somehow that made me feel uneasy instead of glad she'd found something to do on her own. I thought of Ryan's everlasting reminder not to borrow trouble and shook it off.

"It's time for this to wind down," Steve said. "So I'm ready to call it a night."

I nodded. "There's someone else I need to talk to first."

The Córdovas waved goodnight, while Ryan looked at me quizzically.

I took his hand. "It's Sir Lostalot. Here he comes now. With Mrs. Prettypenny in tow."

He'd shed his wig, revealing a full head of auburn hair. The strawberry-blonde beside him had wiped off her stage makeup, replacing it with just a touch of her own cosmetics. She had a kind smile that touched her clear blue eyes. Both appeared to be in their early thirties.

"Thanks for waiting," Sir Lostalot said. "By the way, in real life, I'm Darryl Taylor, and this is my wife, Brenda."

Ryan and I introduced ourselves in turn.

"Darryl and I are involved in the Interfaith Teen Center here in town," Brenda said. "That's how we came to know Keziah."

"Something about her picture drew me to her," I said, which was true, if not the whole truth. "I couldn't help wondering how she happened to go missing."

Darryl glanced around the room. "Let's talk. Maybe tomorrow? Looks like they're trying to hustle us out of here so they can clear away the tables."

"Let me give you our cell-phone numbers," Ryan offered, pulling a card out of his wallet and handing it to Darryl. "We'll be wandering in and out of the local businesses tomorrow, tracking down clues. Anyway, our time is pretty flexible."

Brenda grinned. "I almost forgot about that quasi-scavenger hunt they send you on. Giving you cryptic little notes to find businesses that will give you more cryptic notes."

I smiled too. "Put them all together and maybe we'll figure it out."

"Good luck. I mean that. I hope you're the ones to solve the mystery." Sadness filled her eyes. "I wish the mystery surrounding Keziah would be solved too."

I felt a reflexive intake of breath.

Ryan put his arm around my shoulders. "It's been a long day—for all of us I bet."

"You're right," Darryl said. "It's been hectic. Fun, but hectic. We'll look forward to seeing you tomorrow."

* * *

As I lay wrapped in Ryan's arms and his love, every other thought vanished. I slept soundly—until about 5:00 in the morning, when the events of yesterday began wheeling around my mind like a fast-spinning kaleidoscope. Except that kaleidoscopes form patterns, and nothing fit together in my head.

I got out of bed and bundled up in my robe to ward off the chill. Earlier I'd found a book in the gift shop about Rebecca, the resident ghost. The story beckoned.

The more I read, the more intrigued I became. The clang of the alarm clock jerked me back to the present.

"Who sets an alarm clock on vacation?" Ryan mumbled. "And how come you're already out of bed?"

"We wanted to get an early start on the 'scavenger/clue' hunt. Remember?"

He stretched, then rolled out of bed. "I'll need an early start on the caffeine before I can get an early start on anything else."

* * *

I expected to see Alvina when we met the Córdovas at Rebecca's, the Lodge's only dining room, an inviting combination of elegant and informal. The room was graced by a long row of windows facing the same picturesque landscape of snow-draped evergreens we'd enjoyed yesterday evening. Bronn Journey's harp melodies played softly in the background.

"I am starting to get worried," Cat said. Although her worry seemed out of place in our pleasant surroundings, it transmitted itself to me.

Before we could discuss it further, our hostess seated us. Diane, our server, promptly brought us coffee along with the menus. We forgot Alvina momentarily while we mulled over our choices.

"Would it be possible for me to order something from the dessert menu?" I asked Diane when she returned to take our order. "I've never had Bananas Foster for breakfast, and that kind of appeals to me."

Her brown eyes twinkled. "Sure. Why not?"

After everyone else had ordered, Cat returned to her concerns about her aunt. "She wasn't in her room when we got back last night. I left her a message to call me this morning, but haven't heard anything. Of course, if she came in late, she might be sleeping in."

"Where would she go?" I asked.

"I don't have any idea. She does have her own car, so there's no reason she should be tied down here."

"But it seems odd," Steve said, "after sticking to us like glue, that she'd just take off without a word."

"Well, she did say *something*. But it didn't make much sense."

I nodded. "About chasing ghosts? I wonder what that meant."

"The only thing I could think of, there is supposed to be a ghost that haunts The Lodge."

"Ye-es, but...with Alvina it was probably just a figure of speech," I said. "She seems too pragmatic to take much stock in other-worldly beings."

Cat blushed. "You'll think I'm silly, but I took her at her word. Anyway, I made Steve go with me up to the bell tower first thing this morning. To see if maybe she'd gone up there and fallen or something. Those stairs are steep."

"I don't think you're silly at all. Especially if it put your mind at ease. And—to tell you the truth—I'm a believer. I've been reading about the sassy Rebecca and would welcome a chance to meet her."

"Cool, as our nephew would say," Ryan said. "In the meantime, let's see if we can locate Alvina."

Strange how the person we'd all wished would go away we now wished would come back.

CHAPTER 7

Coming from South Texas, I seldom had a chance to wear heavy winter clothes. So as a pre-Christmas gift, and especially for this trip, Ryan's mom had given me a beautiful Norwegian sweater with an intricate blue and white snowflake pattern. Blue wool pants completed the outfit. I could hardly wait to wear it, and—I confess—to show it off. The morning chill made this the perfect time.

Before we left the lodge, Cat called her mother to see if she might have heard from Alvina.

"Don't worry," her mother had told her. "She's simply not used to reporting in to anyone. She probably went down to El Paso to see Cousin Mela."

Cat might have found this reassuring, but I was skeptical.

"Are Alvina and your mother close?" I asked Cat as we walked to the van.

She shook her head. "Hardly."

Cat didn't seem inclined to elaborate, and I couldn't think of a tactful way to bring up all the questions that flooded my mind. If Cat's mom was so unconcerned about Alvina's disappearance, why had she saddled Cat with watching out for the wretched woman in the first place?

"I like your Aunt Fiona. Does your mom have any other sisters—or brothers?"

"No—there are just the three sisters. Mom's the oldest, Fiona's next, Alvina last."

Cat clammed up again, and we reached the van in silence, Ryan and Steve in animated conversation behind us.

Although I liked Fiona, I felt rather neutral toward Cat's mother. What was her name anyway? Maureen? Cathleen? Doreen? I'd never thought of her as anything but "Mrs. Chikiris." She'd never suggested anything else. Warm toward her family, but somewhat standoffish otherwise. Well, at least Fiona and Mrs. C. seemed normal. What had caused Alvina to be so unlike her sisters—to have such a distorted outlook on life?

"Ryan was telling me about meeting the couple who knew Keziah Porter," Steve said after we'd gotten inside the van and buckled up.

"I hope they call us," I said.

Cat perked up. "What's this all about?"

I told her about meeting the Taylors last night and the possibility of getting together sometime today.

"I thought Keziah's name might have come up last night while we were wandering around meeting the actors," Cat said. "But everyone was pretty focused on the play."

"I thought so too," Steve said. "But I expect most of the people there were probably out-of-towners like us and not up on local happenings."

"It's sad," I said, looking out the window and feeling a tightness in my throat. "In a big city, you get used to seeing flyers like that. Whenever I do, I usually stop and say a quick prayer. But then I put it behind me and go on my way. This is the first time it seems personal."

"We don't know for sure it was Keziah we found," Cat murmured.

"Even if it wasn't, I figured by last night it would be common knowledge that *someone* was found on that mountain. I tried asking 'Mrs. Feelbad,' but I think she resented my fishing. If Her-Brother-The-Sheriff told her anything, she sure didn't share it with me."

Cat turned red. "I fished too. She told me I was the third person to ask."

"If it makes you feel any better, I was the second. I suspect Alvina was the first."

"Well, that would have turned her off for sure."

"Here we are," Steve said, pulling into a parking slot on a side street, after circling the block a couple of times.

There wasn't much traffic on this street yet, so we got out and stood on the sidewalk in front of Astra's Crystals while we looked at our maps. Astra was just opening her shop, and she waved at us through the window. We waved back, then put away our maps and made plans to split up for our search and meet for lunch.

"Ernie's Hot Dogs and Burgers again?" Ryan asked.

"Oh, gosh. With so much going on, I'd almost forgotten," I said.

"Did you even look for those guys we saw at Ernie's while you were milling around last night?"

"Are you kidding? It never crossed my mind."

Steve chuckled. "I *did* look around."

"Figures," Cat said. "You were the only one who thought they might be actors. Did you see anyone?"

"Nah. No such luck. Well, maybe there was one guy before the thing started. Some guy watching the tree being decorated."

My eyes widened. "Really? Which one?"

"The milquetoast one. But I just caught a glimpse of him, and then he left the room."

I frowned. "If he really is a pervert—well, here goes another stereotype—I'd expect him to stay in a sleazy motel, not someplace nice like The Lodge."

"Point taken. I couldn't be sure anyway. But they did look alike."

"Well, we'd better get started. Maybe we'll see them again—but at someplace besides Ernie's."

We agreed on Big Daddy's, then went our separate ways.

It wasn't till my fifth stop, Maribel's Boutique, that I picked up any gossip. Two matronly women were leaning on the counter, carrying on a lively conversation with Maribel. They glanced at me, then went back to their discussion.

Maribel, a petite brunette I guessed to be mid-twentyish, excused herself to ask if I needed help finding something. I smiled and asked about the clue she was to give out.

"Oh, yes." She returned to the counter and pulled out an envelope containing the clues. She handed me a slip of paper with an obscure message on it.

I stared at it for a few moments, then shook my head. "I'm afraid I'm not very good at this."

"Don't worry, It's a little unclear at first. But when you put it together with the other messages, it'll start to make sense."

I brightened. "Thanks for the encouragement." I scanned the shop with its chic clothing, jewelry, and other accessories. "You have some beautiful things. Maybe I should take time out to look around before I get started back on this treasure hunt."

"Please do. Let me know if I can help you."

I busied myself looking through an assortment of scarves, examining each in detail, holding one up now and then. The women turned back to their conversation.

"As I was saying, Hetty, they found that girl right on Ventosa Peak. About a dozen people in those noisy snowmobiles. Ran right over her."

I gulped. *Snowmobiles? A dozen people?* "Um, I'm sorry to butt in, but I couldn't help overhearing. Somebody got run over?"

"Yes indeed," Hetty answered. "Local girl. Well, she really lives—lived—over in Weed."

"What a horrible accident!"

"Oh, it was no accident," the other woman put in, pleased to be one-upping me.

"Someone ran over the girl on purpose?"

"No. Not that. She was already dead when those snowmobilers found her. If you ask me, they ought to ban those things."

I shook my head. "It's a shame."

I hadn't intended to buy anything, but I found a scarf with rosy swirls that would go well with one of the Eileen Fisher dresses I'd bought at Goodwill (price tag still attached). I brought the scarf to the counter to pay.

One of the women turned to me. "So you're here for that mystery theater?"

"Yes. I'm enjoying the weekend. To tell you the truth, I don't particularly care whether I solve the puzzle or not. It's just nice to be here."

She beamed at me. "Well, I hope you do solve it!"

"Thanks. That's very kind of you."

The two women picked up their purchases and headed for the door. Maribel put my new scarf in a fancy box and handed it to me with an invitation to stop in again.

"Whatever you overheard in here," she said with a wink, "I hope you'll take with a grain of salt."

I winked back. "I already did."

CHAPTER 8

Darryl Taylor called right after lunch and asked Ryan and me to come over. Cat and Steve dropped us off at the Taylors' home on Sparrow Avenue, just down the hill from The Lodge.

Darryl greeted us, hung our coats in the hall closet, and led us into the living room. Both Taylors were clearly distraught, Darryl's face pinched and grim, Brenda's pale and streaked with tears. She sat huddled in the corner of a loveseat, with a pastel multi-colored afghan draped across her knees.

To our surprise, Sgt. Tom Alderete was there also, standing by the fireplace. He seemed equally surprised, but merely folded his arms across his chest and waited for the Taylors to set the tone.

Now that I could see his face without the sunglasses and fur hat, I realized he was much younger than I'd thought at first. Twenty-fiveish? Good-looking too, in a subtle rather than flashy way. Light brown hair, with deeper brown eyes.

Darryl made introductions, and we murmured polite hellos.

"Please, have a seat," Darryl said, indicating the sofa, angled toward the matching loveseat.

Sgt. Alderete continued standing. Ryan and I sat down, while I took in our surroundings. The living room was simply but attractively furnished in varying shades of green, accented with pale gold and orange. We were seated on antique white-pine couches with hunter-green cushions.

On the end table next to Brenda was a framed picture of a smiling family—Brenda, Darryl, and three little boys. Judging from his lack of teeth, I guessed the middle one to be about seven. The other two were about a year or so either side of that. Some Legos were off to the side of the room in various stages of construction. Otherwise, I didn't see any sign of the children.

"Would anyone like coffee?" Darryl didn't wait for an answer but headed for the kitchen. I thought he seemed too wound up for coffee, but understood his need to do something—anything—to keep from sitting still.

Since I'd met Brenda only recently, I didn't know if hugs were in order. But she looked so bereft, I couldn't help going to her side and putting my arm around her. She leaned her head on my shoulder for a few moments, then reached for a Kleenex on the end table and wiped her eyes.

"They found Keziah," she said, her voice ragged.

"I know."

"She didn't have many friends her age, and only a few other people seemed to care. You two and Tom. And her sister. But we can't find her."

Alarmed, I looked up at Sgt. Alderete. "Is she missing too?"

"No," he answered. "Not—not like that. She's just not home." He shook his head slightly, and I didn't pursue it.

"We had to identify Keziah," Brenda continued. "Her parents refuse to cooperate. They refused to even acknowledge that she was their daughter." A spark of indignation spurred Brenda to sit up straighter and regain her poise. I gave her shoulder a squeeze, then moved to sit beside Ryan again.

Darryl returned with a large tray holding a carafe of coffee, several mugs, sugar and creamer. He set the tray on the coffee table, with an invitation to help ourselves. I was the only one to take him up on the offer, and then only because it seemed rude to ignore his gesture of hospitality.

I sat down, stirred creamer into the brew, and forced myself to take a few sips. For all I knew, it was gourmet coffee, but my sense of taste had deserted me.

Darryl sat next to Brenda, then stood up again, started to say something, changed his mind, and began pacing.

"So when Keziah's parents wouldn't help, that's when you and Darryl were called?" I asked Brenda, bringing us back to our conversation.

"Yes. Tom told the authorities we'd been trying to help her. We were stunned when we got the call. We bundled up the kids and took them over to my parents', then went to the morgue." Brenda shuddered. "Keziah looked... different...but still...we knew. Even without the birthmark. She had a strawberry birthmark on her neck. She tried to hide it with makeup. Her mother would scrub it off and call her names, and...."

Darryl stopped fidgeting, sat next to his wife and pulled her close. "It's over now."

"Maybe I should tell you...." I looked at Sgt. Alderete, and he nodded. Still, it was hard to find the right words. "I guess you were told how she was found?"

"Some skiers on vacation," Darryl said.

Ryan, who'd been quiet up till now, took a deep breath. "That would be us."

Brenda's eyes narrowed. "So you already knew when you talked to us last night?"

I shook my head. "We didn't know who it was. It was—" I swallowed hard— "very upsetting. Finding someone like that. It's still hard to talk about."

Sgt. Alderete stepped in, gesturing toward us. "I could tell just by looking at you and your friends that you were all pretty rattled."

Brenda's face softened as fresh tears pricked her eyelids.

"Later, when we saw the posters," Ryan said, "we thought there might be a connection."

"And even if the connection was all in our minds," I said, "Keziah became real to us.... I'm not explaining this very well."

Brenda smiled at me. "I think you are."

"We'd still like to know more about Keziah," Ryan said. "But it's been a pretty rough morning for you—"

"No, no," Darryl interrupted. "I mean, yes. But don't go." He and Brenda exchanged glances.

"Rumors will resurface," she said, "and we'd rather you heard about her from us."

Sgt. Alderete looked down. "Maybe I should go now."

"I wish you'd stay," Brenda said. "I know we've already taken up a lot of your time, but—"

"Your perspective would help," Darryl added, his voice gentle but persuasive.

The deputy accepted their invitation and sat down, choosing the recliner, which faced us and helped form sort of a circle.

Now that we were all seated and ready to listen, silence settled in.

Then—as sometimes happens in situations like this—everyone started talking at once.

The ice broken, we laughed, then became somewhat subdued again.

"I'll start if that's okay," I said. "Sgt. Alderete—"

"Please, call me Tom."

"Thanks. Tom. Well, rumors have already started. Just this morning, I heard a highly imaginative account about how Keziah was found."

Tom watched me intently. "And what did you say?"

I spread my hands out, palms upward, and shrugged. "Nothing. It wasn't important enough to contradict. And I didn't want to become part of their gossip. Anyway, I wondered when the news had come out—officially—and how much was made public."

"Well, I can tell you," Tom said, "we appreciate your keeping quiet till Sheriff Gibson was ready to make an announcement. You might have heard him on the radio this morning? Local station."

"No," I said. "We didn't turn on the radio at all."

"It was pretty short and to the point. He said that Keziah had been found dead and thanked people for their efforts to help, or words to that effect."

"He didn't say *how* she was found?" Ryan asked.

Tom's jaw tightened. "Nope."

Remembering Deputy Roy Hendrix's thoughtless remark yesterday when we'd discovered the body, I suspected he liked sounding important and was more than likely the one who gave out details (that got lost in the retelling).

Brenda looked on the verge of tears again. I wondered if she was also on the verge of shock.

"You're sure you feel like going into this today?" I asked. "We can come back tomorrow or even Monday."

She shook her head. "It's not going to get any easier."

Darryl got up and poured them both coffee, stirring a heaping amount of sugar into hers. "It can still wait, sweetheart." The concern was evident in his eyes and in the slow easy way he waited on her.

Brenda smiled up at him as she reached for her coffee. "I'll be okay. Promise."

Darryl started to sit, then half-stood. "Anyone else for coffee? I'm afraid I'm not being a very good host."

Ryan grinned at him. "You made us feel at home when you told us to help ourselves. So that's what we'll do."

Ryan put action to words by pouring coffee for himself. Tom followed suit and eventually we were all in place again. Not wanting another awkward silence to come over us, I plunged right in with my questions.

CHAPTER 9

"Do you know what happened between Keziah and her parents?" I asked. "Why they'd deny she was their daughter?"

Brenda pulled herself together. "I wasn't aware of any 'one-last-straw' thing, if that's what you mean. But there were ongoing problems."

"Were her parents abusive? Was child welfare called?"

"Yes and yes."

"It wasn't as black and white as Brenda makes it sound," Darryl said. "The abuse was emotional rather than physical. And CYFD didn't get involved till the kids suddenly quit going to school."

Brenda reached for another Kleenex and dried her tears. "Darryl is putting it very nicely. When letters and phone calls were ignored, someone from the truancy division went to the Porters' place in person. Mrs. Porter met the poor man at the door with a shotgun, ranting about 'g'mint innerference,' and told him to get off their property."

"*Mrs.* Porter? Where was *Mr.* Porter. That sounds more like something a man would do.... Sorry, gentlemen," I amended.

Tom gave a crooked grin. "You'd think so."

"How long ago was this?" Ryan asked.

"About eight, nine years ago, but that was just the beginning of their run-ins with the truancy folks," Tom said.

"You say the kids quit going to school. How many kids were there?" I rubbed my temples with my fingertips, picturing a run-down shack full of hollow-eyed, shabbily clad children. "You must think we're bombarding you with a lot of questions, but we're just trying to figure out how Keziah fits in the picture."

"They're good questions," Darryl assured us. "And I think the answers are all connected somehow. Tom, you might be able to fill in some blanks here."

"I'll try. To answer your questions one by one—well, maybe not in order—Mr. Porter is just as hostile as his wife. But he's partially paralyzed—result of an automobile accident. So she gets to be the one waving the gun around. They got a huge settlement, plus he gets a pension of some kind. Long and short of it, he never had to go to work again, and they seem to scrape by okay."

"How long ago was the accident?" I asked.

"Maybe twelve, thirteen years ago. Keziah was just a baby. It's all stuff I learned later. Mostly from her sister, Jemma." Tom paused, and gazed off into the distance.

"Anyway," he continued, turning back to Ryan and me, "there were only two kids. Jemma and Keziah. When Jemma was in fifth grade and Keziah in first, that's when they dropped out of school."

"You see, the family lives in a remote canyon that gets snowed in every winter." Brenda said. "So Mrs. Porter decided to home-school the girls."

"That's legal though, isn't it?"

Brenda nodded. "Yes, as long as certain standards are met. But Mrs. Porter hadn't even bothered to tell anybody. Thus began the running battle with the education department."

"The upshot was that the Porters' so-called lesson plans for fifth-graders didn't meet the criteria," Tom said.

"I think I'm getting the picture," I said. "Jemma must have gone back to public school. Was Keziah allowed to stay home?"

"Yes, for a while," Tom said. "Mrs. Porter dug in her heels, and some kind of compromise was made. Keziah got to be home-schooled through fourth grade. As for Jemma, since she hadn't been out of the system more than a few weeks, it was fairly easy for her to make the transition back to public school. It was the best thing that could have happened for her—and for my sister."

"Your sister?"

"Cindy. She's a lot younger than I am. Number Four down the line. She and Jemma got to be good friends, spent a lot of time at our place."

"I guess your sister was a good influence on Jemma."

"Yeah. I think so. But it worked both ways. We have this great big huge family—" Tom spread his arms out as far as they'd stretch "—and everybody is always in everybody else's business."

Ryan and I exchanged a mutual *sounds-like-our-family* look.

"Cindy used to gripe that she couldn't even sneeze without Tía Lupe or Tía Ramona or some other relative 'tattling' to our mom. But when she compared her life to Jemma's, she decided she wasn't so bad off."

"Are the girls still close?"

"They're still friends. One of those things—they don't see each other for a while, then pick up where they left off. Jemma left home and moved to Alamo the minute she turned eighteen. Cindy's going to school in Las Cruces. New Mexico State."

"Alamo?"

"Alamogordo." He grinned. "Not the one you're supposed to remember."

I smiled back. "From now on, I'll remember both. Anyway, it sounds like they have the kind of friendship that, well, I'd guess that Jemma would have turned to Cindy when Keziah disappeared."

"You're right. Cindy came home that weekend. They gave us the only helpful leads we had—"

My cell phone picked that moment to ring.

It was Cat, anxiety in her voice. "I don't know how to break this...."

My fingers tightened on the phone. "Go on."

"Aunt Alvina is in a hospital in El Paso."

CHAPTER 10

Ordinarily I'd have excused myself and continued Cat's call in another room. But I was too floored to move. *Alvina in the hospital?*

"Are you going down to El Paso?" I asked. *Of course they were.* "Would you like us to come with you?"

"I really would...that is, if you don't mind."

"Not at all."

"I'm sorry to interrupt your visit with the Taylors."

"Don't give it another thought. Where are you right now?"

"At the Lodge. We can swing by for you in a couple of minutes. Would you like to come back here before we leave town?"

"I'm not sure. Let me check with Ryan. But come ahead and pick us up."

Everyone looked alarmed, not sure what to make of the one-sided conversation they'd heard.

I apologized, then explained that we needed to go to the hospital with our friends. "They're on their way here right now."

Darryl brought us our coats. "If you think of anything we can do to help out, let us know. Anything at all."

We barely had time to thank them and say our goodbyes when the van pulled up.

Brenda joined us at the door and gave me a hug before we left.

Tears stung my eyes. Not for Alvina, I'm afraid, but for the spontaneous unquestioning concern of the Taylors.

"Do you need to go back to The Lodge for anything first?" I whispered to Ryan, somewhat belatedly, as we approached the van.

"Depends on how long we stay there, I guess."

"I hadn't even thought of that."

"Don't worry, honey. We'll figure it out," Ryan said as he opened the van door for me.

Cat had moved to the back seat so we could sit together, while the men sat in front. Steve took the curving highway into Alamogordo at a careful pace. Still, Cat's nails dug into her palms as she stared out the side window, taking in a sharp breath every time we rounded one of those curves. "This road didn't bother me on the way up here. I don't know why it makes me so jumpy now."

I reached over and patted her hand. "It's natural. I feel a little wired myself."

"Thank you for being here—especially on such short notice."

"What on earth happened to your aunt?"

"We don't know too much ourselves. What she was doing in El Paso is anybody's guess. Cousin Mela didn't know anything about it. Anyway, she was in a car wreck...."

Cat leaned forward and tapped Steve on the shoulder. "What's the name of that hospital we're going to?"

"Thompson something, I think—Thomason? I'll get a map when we get to Texas. GPS has sent me on a few wild-goose chases, so I don't rely on it."

Cat sat back. "My mom didn't have all the details, but it sounded pretty serious."

"When did it happen?"

"Sometime late last night."

"Someone from the hospital called your mom?"

"No. Well—" Cat gave a short laugh. "It was so 'Aunt Alvina' in a way. Maybe that's a good sign. She didn't let anyone in the family know. Instead she called her insurance agent. About her car it seems. And she didn't call him till this morning."

"So how did your mother find out?"

"Apparently Mr. Hopper—he's the insurance guy—Mr. Hopper was worried about her and told her if she didn't call Mom, he would. The fact that Aunt Alvina gave in without arguing told Mom that she must be in pretty bad shape after all." Cat blinked back tears. "I know my aunt's hard to get along with, but I don't like to think of her hurt like that."

"Neither do I."

The road straightened out as we approached Alamogordo, and once Steve had gotten through town, he picked up speed on the freeway into El Paso.

Shortly after we crossed the state line, we stopped at the Welcome Center to get a city map. We spread it out on a long table and all bent over it, pondering the maze of lines and zig-zags leading to the hospital.

Seeing our perplexed looks, the lady behind the counter offered to give us specific directions. After she pointed out the best route to take, she wished us luck and sent us on our way.

What we hadn't counted on was the sheer volume of city traffic. In addition to my frazzled nerves over that, I'd conveniently forgotten I'm one of those people with an aversion to hospitals. By the time we reached the parking lot, I had serious doubts about coming along on this trip.

I'd also forgotten that the climate was milder once we were out of the high mountains. Even though I'd taken off my coat, perspiration beaded my forehead, causing my curls to plaster themselves to my face. "If I didn't think I'd get arrested, I'd take off my sweater too."

"Are you okay?" Cat asked, taking my hand, which felt cold and clammy. "How can you be too warm?"

I smiled half-heartedly. "I'm fine. I feel about unfamiliar busy streets the same way you do about curvy ones."

Ryan opened the back door for us, and as soon as I stepped out, he put his steadying arm around me. "Why don't you wait in the lobby while we figure out where to go. We'll bring back some Cokes."

"I'll wait with you," Cat said, unconvinced that I was "fine."

No one else wanted a soft drink, so Ryan and Steve went off to find one for me. By the time they came back from the information desk and the vending machine, I'd begun to regain my bearings.

There was no mistaking Alvina's room. As we neared the door, we could hear her airing her displeasure at being in "this hellhole."

CHAPTER 11

We found Alvina sitting up in bed, pillows propped at her back. Her face was bruised, large dark circles around her eyes, and her left arm was in a sling. At least she wasn't connected to an array of wires and tubes.

A doctor was standing at the foot of her bed, apparently unfazed by her outburst. He was young, tall, with an athletic build and a blond crew-cut. His arms were at his side, with a medical chart held loosely in one hand.

On seeing us, Alvina growled, "What are *you* doing here?"

Cat moved to her aunt's side and gave her a light hug. "We were worried about you, Aunt Alvina."

"So I see," she responded in a vain attempt to sound gruff.

Watching this unexpected change in her manner, I wondered if she was not used to being hugged and if she was secretly pleased to see Cat, if not the rest of us.

"You're a relative?" the doctor asked Cat, who introduced us all around.

"Your aunt is very independent," the doctor said, "and I can tell she's not used to being, ah, immobilized."

"Don't talk about me as if I'm not here!" Alvina barked, back to her old self. "Whatever you have to say you can say to me directly."

"I've been trying."

The doctor had a disarming smile that kept his words from sounding sarcastic. Personally, I knew how Alvina felt about getting left out of the discussion. But I also sensed the "discussion" had been one-sided, with Alvina's side not listening.

"Your determination to get well is a factor in your favor," the doctor said. "But—" He held up his hand to forestall Alvina's objection. "Your body has undergone a lot of trauma, and you need to give yourself more time to heal."

"I can heal just fine someplace else. I told you, my cousin Mela is on her way here now."'

The doctor looked at Alvina's chart and shook his head. "I can't in all conscience discharge you."

"You can't lock me up either."

He smiled and saluted her, said goodbye to the rest of us, and left the room.

"What's this about Cousin Mela?" Cat asked.

"Your mother has been very busy," Alvina retorted. "But in this case it's a good thing. Good thing she called Mela. Mela will either help me get a rental car or take me back to The Lodge herself."

If Alvina insisted on going back to The Lodge, it would make more sense for us to be the ones to take her. But my heart sank at the prospect. Not only at the thought of being shut up in the van with her for a couple of hours, but at the very real possibility that she wasn't well enough. And if she should have a relapse, it would mean carting her down here again. I silently voted for Mela, whoever she was.

Cat was quiet awhile before speaking, and I suspected she was mulling over the same scenario.

"Don't you think," she said at last, "don't you think it would be better to give yourself another day or two to recuperate—if not here, at Cousin Mela's?"

"Nobody asked you." The words were typical, but the bite was missing.

"Tell me about the accident. What happened?"

I half-expected Alvina to tell Cat it was none of her business. Instead she became more alert, as if welcoming the chance to talk about it.

CHAPTER 12

Before Alvina could say anything more, Mela burst into the room. (Some people enter a room; Melina Constantine bursts.) Of course I didn't know anything about her right away, but I took a good guess. I also guessed her to be about the same age as Alvina (60-something?), but the difference in their appearance set them poles apart.

While Alvina was plain and drab, Mela was colorful to the point of gaudiness: Too-black hair piled high on her head, enough mascara to make a raccoon jealous, and bright red lipstick that reminded me of those big wax lips they sell at Halloween.

She wore a pantsuit of some kind of shiny black and gold material. (*Au courant*, I'm sure, which I confess I'm not.) Pointy shoes with spike heels, dangly turquoise earrings and a large—undoubtedly expensive—squash-blossom necklace completed the ensemble.

On seeing Cat, her eyes widened. "Caterina darling!"

Mela wrapped Cat in an effusive hug, and my initial impression dissipated. I saw only warmth and genuine affection between the two. Even Steve grinned as she wrapped him in a bear hug. Cat introduced Ryan and me and we got Mela-hugs too, though less overwhelming.

Mela pulled up a chair next to Alvina and gave her a quick hug before she could protest.

"Now, Allie, what's this all about? What are you doing here?"

Allie?

"Well, as I was about to explain before I was so rudely interrupted...."

"Tsk, tsk, and I'm going to interrupt again," said Mela, unabashed. "Doreen told me all about the mystery weekend, so you don't need to go into that. I mean, what are you doing *here*? In this hospital?"

"My sister didn't tell you *all* about the weekend. She didn't tell you about the pervert we ran into."

"Oh my, no!"

Alvina nodded smugly. "Well, we first saw him at this hamburger place. Tall, skinny twerp. Then last night I saw him again."

Cat gasped. "You did? Last night? Steve thought he saw him too!"

Alvina regarded Steve shrewdly. "In disguise?"

Steve shrugged. "He looked pretty much the way we'd seen him before."

Alvina waved Steve's sighting away. "Couldn't have been the same person. The man I saw was wearing a mustache. Pretty good fake too. And he'd taken off his glasses. But he couldn't fool me."

"He wasn't one of the actors, was he?" I asked, thinking of Professor Skinflint with his pasty face. But even in retrospect I could see only a passing resemblance between the professor and the nondescript man we'd seen at Ernie's.

"No," she answered impatiently. "It didn't take me long to figure out the villain in that stupid play, so I stepped outside to have a cigarette. And that's when I saw him. Skulking around in the shadows."

"You...uh...saw him that clearly? I mean, with the fake mustache and everything?"

She glared at me. "Plain as day. He was smoking too, and I saw him plain as day when he lit up."

Mm hmm. Plain as day. By the light of a match. In the shadows. In the dark of winter.

"He bolted as soon as he saw me. Recognized me too, I guess. So I bolted right after him."

"You followed him all the way to El Paso?" Cat asked in awe.

"You bet. Straightened out some of those curves on the way to Alamogordo."

Cat shivered. "I can believe that! But you did leave a few."

"Did you catch up with him?" Ryan asked. "Is he the one who caused the accident?"

"No, I lost him once we hit town. He must know these streets, and I don't. Nobody knows how to drive in this city. Idiots going in every which direction. I had the right-of-way too."

I figured from this garbled account that's when the wreck occurred.

"How awful!" Cat said. "Did...did you have wait long for help to come?"

For a change, Alvina was quiet.

"We're tiring you out," Mela said. "We'll give you a chance to rest and come back later."

Alvina rallied. "No! I want you to get me out of here, Melina. If you don't, I'll take a taxi."

"Don't be ridiculous," Mela said.

I suggested the rest of us leave the room while they duked it out, so to speak. At the same time, I wished I could be the proverbial fly on the wall.

CHAPTER 13

"You asked earlier about my family," Cat said in a low voice as she and I sat across from each other at a small round table at the far end of the waiting room.

Only one other person was in the room, but at the opposite end. She appeared to be carrying on a monologue on her cell phone, and—since Ryan and Steve had gone in search of coffee—we effectively had the room to ourselves.

"Steve knows I want to talk to you about this, so they won't be hurrying back."

I nodded.

"Didn't you tell me one time," she continued, skirting the subject, "that your mom's side of the family is Norwegian and your dad's Welsh?"

"Yep. Dad's just a regular guy. My mom imagines that we're all descended from Vikings with heroic names, but I suspect if she pursued another line she'd find someone named Nils the Creep married to Bergitta the Guttersnipe."

Cat laughed. "I don't know much beyond my grandparents' generation. All I know is, Mom's side is Irish and Dad's Greek."

"Where does Mela fit in?"

"Mela's only related by marriage. Her husband is my dad's cousin."

"I see. Interesting that she and Alvina seem to be so friendly. They're nothing alike." I felt my face redden.

Cat overlooked my tactlessness. "Understatement. I think one reason Alvina likes Mela is that they're not really related."

"I see," I said again, although I didn't. I wished Cat would get to the point before other people began filling up the waiting room. But it's been my experience that rushing people is usually counterproductive.

Cat picked at imaginary specks on her jeans. "Aunt Alvina's past is one of those hush-hush things nobody ever talks about. Least of all my mother. But Aunt Fiona confided in me one time after Aunt Alvina had been particularly hateful toward me. She'd said a dress I was wearing made me look like a hooker. Something really trivial in hindsight, but it crushed me at the time."

"You don't forget things like that, do you. Your mother didn't say anything?"

"She jumped on Aunt Alvina, and then it turned into a battle over Mom's lack of parenting skills or something ridiculous. Anyway, it was Aunt Fiona who took me aside to help me understand why Aunt Alvina is the way she is."

"I have a feeling it was some deep hurt."

Cat closed her eyes. "I knew you'd understand." When she looked at me again, her face was troubled. "A few years after my mom and Aunt Fiona were born, it was rumored that my grandmother—my *grandmother*—had an affair. When Aunt Fiona told me, I was horrified, but both my grandparents were dead by then, so I guess she figured it was safe to tell. At least I didn't have to face them."

"You say it was just a rumor?"

"Nana always denied it, but my grandfather was bitter enough to believe it. When Alvina was born, he rejected her, swore she didn't look like anyone in his family."

Cat's story opened old wounds for me in unexpected ways. As if a vise had squeezed the breath out of me, I found myself struggling for air. *Get a grip, Sharon. Breathe, breathe*.

The deep breathing calmed me, reminding me not to compare my life with Alvina's. After all, my father adored me, and there was no doubt whose child I was. But my mother.... It wasn't her fault, I told myself. She simply wasn't cut out for parenthood. She wasn't mean, just remote. And I had been blessed with a number of women who'd showered me with motherly affection.... Still, there was that empty space.... I fumbled in my purse for a Kleenex and dabbed away the tears that had caught me off guard.

Cat reached across the table and took my hand. "I don't want to upset you."

"I'm okay. And I would like to understand Alvina better."

Cat clasped her hands together. "The thing is, my grandfather's cruelty didn't stop. He lavished affection on his older daughters and ignored Alvina. Except to let her know she could never do anything right, could never measure up."

"I thought children like that usually try extra hard to please."

"True. She did that for a long time, according to Aunt Fiona. But about the time she hit thirteen or fourteen, she did an about-face."

"That's pretty normal for that age. Being rebellious, I mean."

"In normal circumstances, she'd have probably outgrown it."

I sighed. "Like the rest of us, thank goodness."

"Now that Mom and Aunt Fiona are adults, they have a better grasp of the damage. Now they regret that they didn't understand at the time, weren't kinder. I think of it as some misguided sense of loyalty. Or guilt."

"Has Alvina ever tried to get counseling?"

"Oh god, no. 'Only crazy people see psychologists.'"

"Was she ever married? Or is Piffle her birth name?"

Cat rolled her eyes. "That was her biggest revenge, her biggest slap in my grandfather's face. He thought she should be grateful that he'd fed and clothed her and put a roof over her head. Alvin Piffle is the name of the person she thinks is her father. She was born Sheila Flanagan but had her name legally changed when she turned eighteen."

"Kinda hard to keep that hush-hush."

"I guess it was pretty embarrassing back then. But that was over forty years ago. Now everyone manages to take her behavior in stride. Meaning we ignore it. Mostly. The only time we really notice it is when we're in public. And you know what? I don't know if she enjoys embarrassing us or if it's gotten to be such a habit she doesn't even notice it herself."

"Well, to her credit, it seems she wants to rid the world of 'the bad guys.'"

"She does like to dramatize herself."

"Do you think she really tailed that guy we saw at Ernie's?"

"Who knows. And there are some details of that accident that are a little murky. She never did tell us exactly what happened."

While we were puzzling over this, our husbands joined us. They announced that it was already dark outside—in case we hadn't noticed—and they were ready for dinner.

"Sounds like a good idea to me," I said. "Let's see what's going on with Alvina and Mela first."

CHAPTER 14

We met Mela and Alvina in the hall just outside Alvina's room. Alvina was dressed, her arm still in the sling. She looked pale, the hollows around her eyes more pronounced.

"We reached a compromise of sorts," Mela explained. "We're leaving this place."

"Was the doctor included in this compromise?" Cat asked, her voice mild.

"Pish posh." With a wave of her be-ringed hand, Mela banished the doctor to obscurity. "What does that youngster know!"

"He seemed pretty capable to me," I ventured.

"Stay out of this," Alvina retorted.

Mela stepped between Cat and me, turned and put her arms around us. "I know you're just worried, but I think the best medicine for Allie would be to get her out of here. I'm taking her back up to the Lodge."

"I already told you," Alvina added, less defensively, "I solved the mystery in that play they put on. I need to turn in my solution tonight so I can be there when they announce the winner tomorrow morning."

I supposed if the Córdovas put their clues together with Ryan's and mine, we might be able to make a reasonable stab at the outcome, but—individually—I don't think any of us had collected enough clues.

"Well, you sure outfoxed us," Cat said. "Now tell us about the compromise."

"After the announcements tomorrow morning, I'll take her back home with me and she can finish recuperating," Mela said, returning to stand by Alvina.

"I've been wondering," I said, "about the guy you followed down here. You must have gotten his license number."

"Of course." She didn't add "you idiot," but the thought vibrated in the air. "It was a California plate, and that pervert said he was from California. So it all adds up."

Mela gave us warning glances and patted Alvina's shoulder. "Now, Allie. We can follow up on that later. I have connections," she added obscurely. "Let's get out of here before the prison guards show up."

Without further ado, the two women continued on their way, Mela's heels clicking along the smooth corridor, Alvina's Red Cross shoes plodding along at the same pace.

* * *

"Before we leave town," I said, "I'd like to get the police report on that accident, if possible. Cat, do you have Mela's cell-phone number?"

"I do. Here, use my phone and you can talk to her yourself."

Mela was able to coax the information we needed from Alvina: description and license number of her car, and the approximate time of the accident.

"Allie's more upset about wrecking that car than about taking care of herself," Mela said. "It's fifteen or twenty years old, and she could stand to get a new one, but she'll probably keep it another fifteen or twenty years if it can be salvaged."

After wading through the requisite red-tape, we finally got hold of the report. For all the good it did us. The accident was a hit and run, which wasn't any surprise. Apparently Alvina blacked out right afterwards. Someone called 911, then left the scene. There were no witnesses or even passersby in the area.

* * *

Ironically, we had planned to come to El Paso tomorrow afternoon, spend a little time exploring the city, then see the Córdovas off on a late flight to San Antonio. We'd have to turn in the van; then Ryan and I would rent another car to use during the rest of our stay in Cloudcroft.

Tonight we had dinner at Cappetto's Italian Restaurant, which Mela had recommended.

"Let's eat here again tomorrow," I said as I finished my pasta della casa.

"Breakfast, lunch, and dinner," Cat agreed with a sigh. "I wish we could stay longer. But I'll be glad to see the kids again."

"Me too," Steve said. "I got a text from Heather that she and Josh actually miss us. Even with all the spoiling they're getting from Grandma."

* * *

After leaving El Paso, we arrived back at the Lodge about 10:00. Mela had left a message for Cat, asking for all of us to meet her in the lounge "no matter how late."

Mela was still dressed in her exotic fashion, but her face showed lines of fatigue.

"Allie took a pain pill and is asleep," she said. "All she needs is rest, which she's more likely to get here on her own terms without people traipsing in and out to check on her." Mela laughed. "Except me, of course, but I can peek in from time to time without waking her up. My room is just down the hall from hers."

"I'm glad you were able get something here at the last minute. They're pretty full this weekend," Cat said.

"I called before we left El Paso, in case we needed to move to another place. We were lucky—you're right, there weren't many rooms left. Allie doesn't know it, but I also talked to the doctor. He was mostly concerned about her being alone and being too stubborn to—well, you know Allie."

Mela gave herself a little shake. "That's not why I asked you to call me. Luckily she had only a slight concussion, which is healing as it should. But she does have some temporary memory problems, which the doctor told me is normal. She told me about that man she suspects of being...'the local pervert' is the way she put it. She didn't admit it earlier, but she really wasn't sure if the man she saw smoking is the same one. She followed him in hopes she could find out."

"She said she lost him," I said. "I wonder. If they were going as fast as she says, he must have become a little suspicious himself. Do you think he might be the one who caused the accident?"

"That crossed my mind. One problem is that the accident is a blur for her. The first thing she recalls clearly is the paramedics standing over her. Another 'problem'—if it is one—is that she really doesn't remember the numbers of his license plate. She won't admit that either. Not outright anyway. She'll just say it ended in 242 or 357 or 'something like that'—as if that's all it would take to track it down. She gets a little irritable if you suggest that's not enough."

Irritable? Not our Alvina!

Cat hugged Mela. "I feel better knowing you're here. It's been quite a day, so I hope you'll get some sleep yourself."

Mela's face lit up as she returned the hug. "I intend to, Caterina dear! And now that I'm here, I plan to go to the spa tomorrow. The Lodge is one of my favorite places, and I don't see any need to hurry away."

* * *

"I thought that incident at Ernie's was just coincidence," I told Ryan when we were back in our room. "But now I'm having second thoughts. Now *I* am going to get online and see if I can find that guy among the 'local perverts,' as Alvina calls them."

"Tonight?"

"It shouldn't take that long. There can't be that many around here."

"Might as well. By the way, weren't we going to compare our solutions to the other mystery?"

"Solutions? Ha! I have no solution. How 'bout you?"

"A few guesses. I'd hoped you could help me pin them down."

I felt ashamed. After all, the original purpose of this trip was to get involved in the play. I'd gotten too sidetracked to think about it, but Ryan had evidently gotten into the spirit of the event.

"Let's compare," I said. "I might have actually picked up a clue or two. The *real* bad guys—if any—can wait."

We came up with plausible ideas, wrote them down, then returned to the front desk to turn them in. There we met the Córdovas turning in their own solutions.

"I thought we'd missed the deadline," Steve said as we all walked back toward our rooms. "But we found out that

'Sir Lostalot' called to explain we'd had an emergency and to ask for an extension."

"Now we feel kinda guilty," Cat added. "We'd decided Sir Lostalot was the villain. That's really Darryl Taylor, isn't it?"

"Yes, but don't feel bad," I said. "We voted for Brenda—'Mrs. Prettypenny.' Person least likely, but with plenty of motive. When you think about it, it's really a tribute to their acting skills."

Ryan grinned. "Not that they'll ever know. Alvina's the one who's solved the mystery."

We laughed and wished each other good night. Good while it lasted.

CHAPTER 15

Sunday morning I woke up in the wee hours again. I lay snuggled next to Ryan for a while, with nothing more on my mind than the comfort of his presence. Before long other thoughts clamored for attention, and I remembered I'd wanted to check out the sex-offender site online.

Three a.m. "The witching hour." *Good thing I'm not superstitious.* I slipped out of bed, careful not to wake Ryan, and dressed quickly. I scribbled a note for him and left it on the night table.

Although WiFi wasn't available, a computer for guests' use was set up in the hall near the lobby, and I had picked up the password when we checked in. A couple of advantages to using it in the middle of the night: Not only was The Lodge quiet, but I'd probably have the computer all to myself for as long as I wanted. I logged in and began my Internet search.

After several tries, I turned up a promising site: Registered sex offenders in the Alamogordo area and their supposed addresses. No photos. I tried another site, this one with a number of stamp-sized mugshots. I wondered if people in lineups went out of their way to adopt identical sullen expressions. If Mr. Stetson's wife found anyone she could identify here, she was a better woman than I.

I squinted, wondering if it was time for me to get a pair of those reading glasses at the H-E-B. Then I spotted him. Second line, third from the left: Horace "Bulldog" Waller. If ever there was someone who did NOT look like a bulldog, he was it. He had served a brief sentence for indecent exposure in Pocatello, Idaho. A few months later he'd moved to Tularosa, New Mexico, where his sister lived, and had re-registered there.

The resemblance to the man we'd seen at Ernie's was strong, but who could be sure from looking at a postage stamp?

On impulse, I typed in "Keziah Porter." Before her name even appeared on the screen, I became aware of a sudden current of cold air, causing the little hairs on the back of my neck to rise. Not the kind of draft caused by a door opening or closing, but a chill that seeped into my bones. I sat motionless, listening. A single word sounded softly in my head: *Danger*.

Shaken, I stood and looked around. Had I heard a radio? Part of someone's conversation? I saw no one, heard nothing. I was alone, surrounded only by silence.

CHAPTER 16

Had I imagined it? Did "late to bed early to rise" two days in a row cause something in the brain to snap? To dream up a wave of cold air and a sinister murmur out of nowhere?

I didn't wait to see which websites Keziah's name might have turned up. I logged off the Internet as quickly as possible, then rushed back to our room. Ryan was dressed and had turned up the thermostat. The room was warm and welcoming. Ryan's arms were warm and welcoming.

"What happened to you?" he asked, holding me close and stroking my hair. "You look as if you've seen the mysterious Rebecca."

"I'm not sure."

Ryan was quiet, waiting for me to explain things in my own way.

"I didn't see her," I said, "but I think I might have encountered her."

Ryan tensed, and his arms dropped to his sides. "Let's sit down." After moving the teddy bear out of the way, he helped me get seated in the armchair. Then he pulled the desk chair over so we could sit across from each other, our knees touching. He reached out and held both my hands.

"Do you think I'm hallucinating?" I asked. Part of me was annoyed that he seemed to be patronizing me, and the other part was hoping he could offer a rational explanation.

"No. I don't think that at all. Tell me what happened."

I looked into his sympathetic brown eyes and poured out everything: about surfing the Internet and about the strange sensations I'd experienced.

"Well," he said, "I consider myself a pretty down-to-earth guy. But something weird happened to me too. A voice woke me up. Maybe the same one. All I heard was 'danger.'"

My hands tightened in Ryan's gentle grip.

"I thought I must have been dreaming," he continued, "but I couldn't shake it off. All your note said was 'Back soon' with a little heart. So I was about to come looking for you when you came in the door."

I took a deep breath. "Whatever happened, I'm glad we both felt it. Now we just have to figure out what it means."

Ryan released my hands, then walked over to the window and opened the drapes. The moonlight, dulled by a cloudy sky, could do no more than cast gray misty shadows on the snow below.

"It must have something to do with—Horace Waller," I said. (I couldn't bring myself to call him Bulldog yet.) "Or maybe someone else on that website."

Ryan didn't answer but continued staring out the window.

"Or something not connected?" I murmured.

"Could be. Let's let it go for now. The 'wrap-up' breakfast won't start for a while, but maybe we can get some coffee to hold us over till then."

I swallowed hard. "We'll have to go down that hall again, won't we."

"Either that or stay in this room forever."

I spent a minute or two freshening up, and we started toward the lounge. Neither of us felt anything unusual on the way. The uneasiness we'd both felt vanished, though Ryan still seemed lost in thought.

* * *

We sat at the breakfast table with the Córdovas and Alvina. She grumbled about feeling achy, but when Cat offered to take her back to the hospital, she turned her complaints to the food instead. The rest of us thought the eggs Benedict, cinnamon rolls, and fresh oranges were superb.

As the meal came to a close, the actors came onstage again, this time to reveal the ending to the play. Then the names of those who'd solved the "who, why, how, when, and where" were announced.

The four of us were mildly disappointed, but certainly not surprised, to find that we weren't among the winners. Alvina, on the other hand, was floored to find that all of her answers were wrong.

"Somebody must have switched the numbers. I still think it was that stuck-up Mrs. Feelbad," she muttered as she stomped out of the room.

Once again the actors circulated among the crowd. Louise Gibson, aka Mrs. Feelbad, surprised me by seeking me out.

"I apologize for cutting you off the other night," she said. "And please call me Louise. I don't want to live up to my 'feelbad' persona."

"It's all right. I hadn't meant to put you on the spot."

"You didn't. Someone else did, and I was feeling a little defensive."

"Well, that's understandable."

"I should have given you the benefit of the doubt. Brenda told me later about your concern for Keziah."

"I do feel connected to her somehow." I paused. "Now I *am* being nosy. Do you mind telling me what that other person said that put you off? If she's who I think she is, I know she gets carried away sometimes."

Louise studied me a moment, then smiled. "'Carried away'—how euphemistic. I can probably laugh about it now. Anyway, someone had told her the sheriff is my brother. So she seemed to think I was Second-in-Command. My brother would get a kick out of that. He never tells me anything."

"Probably a good thing."

"I agree. But this woman said she *knew* who was responsible for Keziah's disappearance and why wasn't I doing something about it. If she hadn't been so obnoxious, I might have asked her what she meant."

"The thing is, we did overhear a rather odd conversation. I didn't put much stock in it." I told Louise about the exchange we heard at Ernie's, and about finding "Bulldog" online. "If I could get that information so easily, I'm sure the authorities are aware of it."

"I don't think I've seen your 'Mr. Nondescript' or 'Bulldog' either. But your description of 'Mr. Stetson' could fit any number of people. I can't imagine confronting a stranger like that, though."

"It didn't do much for our appetite."

I noticed that someone else was waiting to talk to Louise, so we ended our chitchat and I stopped to talk with some of the other actors.

Brenda and Darryl waved to me, so I rounded up Ryan and the Córdovas, and we headed their way.

"I was hoping we'd get a chance to meet you," Brenda told Cat and Steve.

"So were we," Cat said. "Yesterday just wasn't a good time—for any of us."

"Understatement! We were all a little frazzled yesterday, I think. How is your aunt, by the way?"

"Much better. In fact, she insisted on, uh, figuring out the ending to the mystery."

"Speaking of figuring out things, should we confess?" Ryan asked, a mischievous gleam in his eyes.

"Oh, by all means. Remember," I told the Taylors, "it's because we were so impressed with your acting, that we all voted for both of you as the culprits."

"Half the fun is fooling people," Brenda said, her blue eyes twinkling, "so your 'confession' made our day."

We chatted amiably for a few more minutes; then the Córdovas excused themselves to check on Alvina.

"You said something about getting together on Monday," Darryl said. "I hope that means you're not leaving just because the play is over."

"No, we're actually spending a couple more weeks here," I said.

The Taylors then explained their own typical routine. Darryl, a CPA, was enjoying a lull before the new year began and tax season got underway. Brenda was a teacher's aide at her sons' school. Two or three afternoons a week they volunteered at the Teen Center they'd told us about, while their boys got to spend time with their grandparents.

"Why don't you two visit us tomorrow afternoon," Brenda said. "You might enjoy seeing how it works, plus you can meet some kids who knew Keziah."

"We'd like that," I said. "Speaking of Keziah, Tom Alderete said something about a helpful lead his sister and Jemma had given them. I'm curious to know what that was."

The Taylors exchanged glances.

"Give Tom a call tomorrow morning," Darryl suggested. "I think he'll be glad to fill you in—and to get your feedback."

CHAPTER 17

Shortly after lunch, we drove to El Paso as we'd originally planned, did some sight-seeing, then went to the airport to make the rental-car transactions.

I felt a little bereft as we saw the Córdovas off. Right now the times we'd shared overshadowed everything else. I hoped we'd be able, one of these days, to remember the fun we'd had making snow angels.

"If you need me, I'm just a phone call away," Cat reminded me as she hugged me goodbye.

*   *   *

On the way back to The Lodge, I made a mental list of the puzzles we'd come across—all of them darting around my mind at random.

Back in our room, I sat cross-legged on the bed and set up my laptop so I could put that list in black and white. I asked Ryan for his help, so he propped pillows against the headboard and leaned back against them.

"I don't know where to start," I admitted. "We have Keziah's death, the 'Bulldog/Mr. Nondescript' mystery, Alvina's accident, and a 'ghostly warning.' Is there any connection?"

"Let's just take them one by one and save the connection for later."

"Good idea."

"First things first. We don't know for sure how Keziah died. Exposure? Hypothermia? Or was she murdered? If it was murder, who killed her? And was it on the mountain, or was she moved there later?"

I typed up Ryan's questions, then added, "And why? Maybe when we talk to the Taylors and Tom Alderete, they'll have some ideas."

Ryan scooted up next to me so he could look over my shoulder. "What's with Keziah's sister?" he asked. "It sounded as if she and Tom's sister were on to something."

I typed in, "Where is Jemma? What does she know? Or suspect?"

"What do Keziah's friends know?"

"Why have her parents cut her off?"

I stopped typing and stared at the computer screen.

"Anything else?" Ryan asked.

"Not off the top of my head. Let's move on." I typed in, "Are Bulldog and Mr. Nondescript the same person? Sex offender or innocent bystander?"

"If they're not the same, it really doesn't matter who Mr. Nondescript is."

"You're right." I paused, then continued typing:

1. Is either man connected to Keziah?
2. Did Alvina really see either of them?
3. If she did, did he cause her accident?

"My opinion—you don't need to put that in here—Alvina's the kind of person who tries to bulldoze people into thinking she's always right. Look at the way she insisted she could solve the mystery play. And couldn't admit she was wrong when it stared her in the face."

"Yeah." I folded my arms and studied the ceiling as if it could supply some insight. "Then again...remember the little boy who cried wolf? Sometimes people like Alvina really are right."

I resumed the list. "Maybe her mind will clear and she'll remember the license number."

Ryan chuckled. "And maybe Sheriff Gibson and his sister will give her the 'Citizen of the Year' award."

I laughed with him. "Okay, you win. Moving right along. What was that mysterious warning all about?"

"Mind our own business?"

"Or follow through. But be careful?"

"Sharon—"

"I know. You're not going to let me out of your sight."

"Darn right." He put his arm around me and kissed me on the cheek. "I'll drag you off cave-man style if I think you're in danger."

* * *

Monday afternoon we took the Taylors up on their invitation to visit the Teen Center. Brenda welcomed us when we arrived, explaining that Darryl was helping a student with a shop project and would join us shortly. Her face reflected her enthusiasm as she showed us around and explained how volunteers from the Interfaith Community had pitched in to build the Center a few years ago.

Once the structure was completed, she told us, the kids themselves had painted the inside walls and found a variety of photos and posters to decorate them. Someone had sewn curtains with red, yellow, and green geometric designs that further adorned the place.

I was impressed with how well organized it was. The building itself was shaped in a long rectangle. Restrooms were situated at either end. Midway along one of the long walls was a small office with a big glass window facing the main door on the opposite side.

"We can keep an eye on things if we need to do paperwork," Brenda said. "*Or* the office offers some privacy if one of the kids needs to talk with us."

A vending machine stood nearby, stocked with various kinds of yogurt and fruit juice rather than pop. Besides the usual array of furnishings—chairs, tables, and bookcases—two pool tables and two ping-pong tables filled one end of the room. Right now, all were occupied. At the other end of the room, I saw a few kids involved in chess games or board games or just chatting. I noticed that no computers or electronic games were in sight.

"No," Brenda said when I asked her about it. "There was quite a discussion about computers and such at the board meetings when we first got started. In the end we all agreed that kids had plenty of access to that stuff other places." She pressed her lips together briefly. When she spoke, her voice was barely audible. "Too many other places."

Darryl strode toward us, all smiles. "What do you think of the tour? Not that any two days are ever alike. We try to have field trips whenever possible—ski trips, ice skating, hiking—even archery in the summertime."

Brenda brightened. "And we have a group that's formed a drama club. They got excited about it after seeing how much Darryl and I enjoyed our stint in community theater."

"They're planning to do *Oklahoma!* Pretty ambitious, but they're excited. You should see the sets they're building."

"Why don't you take Ryan over there?" Brenda suggested. "I'd like to introduce Sharon to some of Keziah's friends.... If that's okay with everyone?"

More than okay. Ryan liked the idea of seeing what the builders were doing. He and Darryl set off for an adjoining structure, where an assortment of lumber, sawhorses, and tools was set up.

And I was curious about Keziah.

CHAPTER 18

Brenda introduced me to another volunteer, Stephania, who was helping one of the teens with her homework. "We'll be in the office for a few minutes," Brenda told her.

Stephania smiled and waved us away. "Take your time."

"You'll laugh when I tell you this," Brenda said, once we were in the office and had hung our coats on the hooks by the door. She rummaged in the bottom drawer of the desk and pulled out a skein of yarn in golden and red hues that brought out the highlights in her hair. Next she took out knitting needles and a foot or two of whatever she was knitting. It hadn't taken on any apparent shape, so I had no clue what it was supposed to be.

"I'm just barely thirty," Brenda said, straightening up, "but I think of myself as the resident Miss Marple. I sit on the couch and knit—I've finished one afghan already. After a while, kids—girls mostly—come sit beside me and tell me things."

A calm, cozy, non-threatening environment. And Brenda, a kind and nonjudgmental confidante.

"Today I'll take the initiative, though," she said. "I'd like to introduce you to the girls Keziah was friendly with. I don't know exactly how close they were, but they did hang out together."

"How are they dealing with her death?"

"Not too well. I talked to them when they first came in this afternoon. We cried together, which helped a little. I didn't ask any questions, and after a while I left them with their own thoughts." Brenda sighed. "Even the ones who didn't know Keziah are having a hard time. Kids tend to think they're immortal, and it's always a shock to discover someone their age has died. Especially under these circumstances."

"How did they react when she first disappeared?"

"That's what's bothering me. Those who didn't know her buzzed about it for a few days, and then got absorbed in their own teen angst. But those girls who knew her hardly batted an eye. I think they know something. Tom thinks so too, and Sheriff Gibson questioned them back then. But it was see nothing, hear nothing, tell nothing."

"That's tough. You think they might change their tune now that she's been found?"

"We hope so. Tom suggested they might be more willing to talk to me than to 'official-looking' people."

"He's right. They're much more likely to confide in Miss Marple. But where do I come in? Won't it put them off to have a stranger show up?"

"I don't think so. I told them you might be coming here today. I didn't go into a lot of detail. Just said you were one of the skiers who'd found Keziah and were as distressed about her death as we were."

"I'm glad you told them. But I'm still a stranger. I hope they don't clam up."

"Don't worry about it. I don't know what to expect myself," she admitted, "with or without you. So it might as well be with you. Besides, I think you're hiding your light under a basket."

"Oh?"

Her fair skin turned pink. "Tom did a little investigating after our meeting. He knew you were a lawyer, and it occurred to him that you might be taking part in that symposium that's coming up. Well, he knows the woman who's coordinating it—Janet Landau. So he asked her about you."

"Oh."

"Please don't take it the wrong way. He was curious, that's all."

I laughed. "I can't throw rocks at anyone for being curious."

"Neither can I. I'm just glad you're here. Janet raved about you. She said, among other things, that you had a knack for dealing with kids."

"My heart does go out to kids."

"So, let's go meet a few. I probably need to start circulating anyway." We left the office, Brenda closing the door quietly behind us.

* * *

In the far corner of the room, three girls about fourteen or fifteen sat close together on a tan leather couch, whispering among themselves. Their books were piled on a card table in front of them.

We strolled in their direction, stopping once to select juice from the machine—apple for Brenda and orange for me—and a second time so she could point out a picture she especially liked. In the meantime, the girls opened their textbooks and made a production of looking deeply absorbed in them.

I'm not sure how much actual reading they were doing and doubt if they were fooled by our subtle approach. But at least we'd given them a chance to ease into the plan.

Brenda smiled at them as if our appearance was their idea all along. "Hi," she said softly. "May we join you?"

They looked at each other and shrugged with varying degrees of boredom—and a slight degree of apprehension.

One girl wore "Coke-bottle" glasses that had slipped down her nose. She studied us a moment over the rims, revealing sad gray eyes. With a quick touch of her forefinger, she slid the glasses up again. Their bright magenta frames seemed out of place with her straight, dishwater-blond hair, making her look vulnerable somehow, younger than her teen years.

"I guess so," she ventured.

"Thanks," Brenda said. She made introductions and we drew up straight chairs on either side of the card table, then sat down to drink our fruit juice. I realized how helpful it was to have our own method of avoiding forced conversation.

After a minute or two, another girl asked in a voice just barely polite, "Are you going to ask us questions about Kezzie?"

I tried not to choke on my orange juice. I guessed the girl to be the Alpha person in this group, brash in both manner and looks. A curtain of bleached platinum hair hung over one eye, while the rest of her hair was short and shaggy. The eye I could see was an unnatural shade of green, thanks to contacts—or one contact, as the case might be.

Brenda side-stepped the question. "I don't want you to tell me anything you're uncomfortable with. But—if you're free to discuss it—I do wonder why Keziah's parents treated her so badly."

"Her mother was horrible!" the third girl offered without hesitation. She had a fresh-scrubbed innocence about her, from her slightly freckled face with its lack of make-up to chestnut brown hair that hung in a neat French braid halfway down her back.

"That's the rumor I heard," Brenda said without inflection.

"It's true!" Wilma, the girl with the thick glasses, insisted. "Have you ever met her?"

"No, I haven't. But it sounds like you might have."

Dot (the one I privately called "Alpha Girl") puckered her lips and blew a blast of air toward the shock of hair covering half her face. The veil lifted briefly before settling again in its accustomed style. "Not like, hello, how do you do. Not that kind of 'met.' But we've seen her around."

Brenda nodded, and I took a sip of my juice.

"She comes down to Alamo to shop," put in Phyllis, the third girl in the group. "My mother talked to her at Lowe's one time. She asked her if Kezzie could come to church with us. You wouldn't believe how she talked to my mom!"

"Duh! I was there, remember?" Dot said. "That woman started talking about hell and how we were all goin' there."

"We're Baptists," Phyllis said. "But my mom said that compared to Mrs. Porter, we're downright hedonists."

I couldn't help laughing. "I like your mom already."

Phyllis smiled for the first time. "I know it's hyperbole—another word I had to look up. But we all know how mean Mrs. Porter treated Kezzie. Always telling her she was no good and stuff like that. Telling her she'd wind up like her sister."

Dot shot Phyllis a warning look. "Her sister's okay."

"Yes, she is," Brenda said. "And so was Keziah."

Phyllis opened her mouth, caught another of Dot's daggered glances, and closed it again.

"I'm going to be very direct," Brenda said in her quiet way. "I think Keziah ran away."

Phyllis squirmed in her chair while Dot studied her black nail polish. Wilma took off her glasses, wiped her eyes on her sleeve, then jammed the glasses back on.

"Don't say anything right now," Brenda continued. "But give it some thought. Now that she's been found, everything's changed."

Dot folded her arms and blew her hair out of her face again. "Why would we tell you anything?"

"I don't know. Why would you?" Brenda reached over and gave each of the girls a quick pat on the arm, even Dot. "I won't bring this up again. Let's change the subject. What can we do to honor Keziah? She liked to paint. Do we have any of her artwork we can hang in here?"

Phyllis looked away. "Her sister might have something. I'll ask her."

"Good. Now I'm going to leave you all to your homework and finish showing Sharon around. She hasn't seen the shop yet."

CHAPTER 19

Brenda made a peace sign, and I followed suit. Then we ambled away, stopping a couple of times to look at some paintings by members of the Teen Center. When we opened the door leading outside, cold air blasted us.

"The shop is just a hop, skip, and jump away, but we can go back for your coat if you'd like," Brenda said.

"Hopping, skipping, and jumping work for me."

Dashing worked too. Perpendicular to the main center, the shop was easy to reach. A converted single-wide mobile home, it had been gutted out to house a motley supply of donated building equipment.

A number of boys—and a few girls—were busy with hammer and saw. Darryl and Ryan were helping a group across the room and didn't notice us come in. Brenda made no move to join them but made a sweeping gesture around the room instead.

"Mostly they're building sets for the musical," she told me. "Which is kind of funny, because we haven't even started rehearsals yet." Despite her cheerful tone, I knew we both felt somewhat deflated.

"Is there someplace where we can sit and finish our fruit juice?" I asked.

"We can sit right here and pretend we're watching them work. I mean, we can *really* watch them too."

Apparently the carpenters were too involved in their projects to take time for sitting. The only chairs available were unpadded folding chairs, so we set up two of them against the nearest wall.

We each had quite a bit of juice left, which I hoped would revive us. "I think we need a little time to process what happened back there."

Brenda took a deep breath. "More pretending on my part, I'm afraid. I acted more confident than I felt around those girls."

I squeezed her hand. "You convinced me."

"Maybe I should have pressed them more. But—talk about the proverbial brick wall—I could almost *feel* my head banging against it."

"You did the right thing. I have to admit, I was kinda disappointed they didn't have any questions for *me*. I thought for sure they'd ask me something. Something that might open up discussion."

"It's odd they didn't. I'm just stymied. I wish I could talk to Phyllis, or even Wilma, away from Dot."

"Do you know what Phyllis meant about Mrs. Porter saying Keziah might turn out like her sister? I got the impression from Tom that Jemma is pretty levelheaded."

"Bingo! Oh, Sharon, you're so funny, and you're not even trying to be. God forbid that Keziah should be levelheaded and think for herself!"

Two girls dressed in paint-spattered sweatsuits trotted over, set up chairs, and plopped down beside us.

"Oh, Ms. T., you wouldn't guess how hard they've been working us!" one of them said, placing the back of her hand against her forehead.

"Yeah, right," said the other one. Then they both began giggling.

Brenda grinned. "Tell me about the hours and hours they've forced you to work."

More giggling. "About thirty minutes," the first girl said. "I did the coneflowers and the black-eyed Susans."

Brenda stood and turned to me. "C'mon, Sharon. Let's go see the fruits of their labors."

Silly as these girls were, there was something refreshing in their silliness. Maybe it was simply the contrast to the brooding atmosphere surrounding Keziah's friends.

We applauded the scene they'd helped paint on a canvas backdrop: chickens and flowers against the side of a red barn. Then we checked on Darryl and Ryan's progress as they nailed canvas to frame, readying it for more paint.

I thought about our own progress, Brenda's and mine. I felt that Brenda had opened a door, if only a tiny crack, and sooner or later the girls would be more forthcoming.

As for me, things I'd heard from the Taylors or Tom Alderete were reinforced. Mrs. Porter was indeed a tyrant. And I'd learned a few things from Phyllis that were new to me. For one thing, Mrs. Porter was not merely anti-social, she was a religious nut as well. No big surprise there.

And Jemma had done something to bring down her wrath. Something more than simply thinking for herself. I was sure of that.

* * *

As Ryan and I walked toward our rented Saturn, I saw Dot standing under a ponderosa, just beyond the Teen Center boundary I supposed. Even in the dusk that was closing in, I could see she was smoking. Without warning, I felt as if I were looking at a mirror of my own chip-on-the-shoulder self back when I was her age.

Whatever it was, my heart softened toward Dot. I smiled and waved. She looked away, dropped her cigarette, and ground it out.

Ryan and I had settled ourselves in the car and fastened our seatbelts when I heard a tap on the window. Dot.

I rolled down the window. "Hey."

She backed up a step or two, then ducked her head so it was level with mine. "Are you coming here again tomorrow?"

"Mm. I think so. Yes. I am."

"Okay. See ya." She turned and walked away.

Well, how about that.

CHAPTER 20

I hadn't planned to go back to the Teen Center the next afternoon, but my encounter with Dot changed that.

Tuesday morning I got up early and made minor shifts in my daily calendar. First of all, I needed to go over the outline I'd prepared for my part in the Symposium on Immigration Law.

As soon as Ryan woke up, I collared him for help. "I'm supposed to show how the immigration system in our country evolved. Would you give me some feedback?"

"Evolved? How far back do you plan to go? The Bering Strait theory?"

"Ha ha. Not the feedback I had in mind." I looked at my notes again. "Okay, I think I'll start by pointing out that immigration laws here didn't even exist until 1875."

"So—your plan is to explain how everything got so complicated over the next hundred-and-something years?"

I sighed. "Three years of law school and fifteen years of experience crammed into thirty minutes."

"Make it personal, Sharon. Tell about *your* immigrant ancestors."

"Oh, right. I wish I had something to tell. I always tune out when my mother starts talking about our family tree. The good news is they came over before legislation to exclude idiots and lunatics."

"What more do you need? Okay, okay. Let me get some caffeine to jump-start my brain, and we can work on it some more later. You have till Thursday, don't you?"

* * *

Registration for the symposium was scheduled throughout Tuesday, with a "meet-and-greet" cocktail hour to take place before dinner. I had registered early—one thing to check off the list. I could go to the Center soon after school let out, hope Dot showed up, and hope to be back at the hotel in time to meet the symposium attendees. Lots of "hoping" here.

We ran into Mela at the breakfast buffet at Rebecca's. She reported that Alvina was feeling better, though still bruised and achy. I was glad Mela had things well in hand; with Cat gone, I had felt some residual sense of responsibility toward her aunt. With that off my shoulders, I gave Tom Alderete a call and set up an appointment with him.

* * *

"Many more trips to Alamogordo, and I can take out some of these curves myself," Ryan said as we zipped down the highway that had become so familiar to us. Despite his words, Ryan was a skillful driver, and I could keep my eyes on the scenery instead of the road.

"Many more trips to Alamogordo, and I might remember to dress in layers." Despite the short distance in miles, the difference in terrain and climate between the mountains surrounding Cloudcroft and the desert surrounding Alamogordo still caught me unawares.

When we arrived at department headquarters, Tom showed us into a small conference room. We accepted his offer of coffee and made ourselves comfortable on dark-blue cushioned armchairs. Sheriff Gibson poked his head inside the door and greeted us before ducking out again.

"I invited Jemma to join us later," Tom said. "I thought you'd like to meet her."

"Yes, I would," I said. "We've wondered how she's holding up."

Tom frowned. "Hard to tell. I wasn't entirely upfront with the Taylors. I called my sister—Cindy—the same afternoon Keziah was found and asked her to come home right away, even though I knew she'd be back for Christmas break in a few days anyway. Thought she'd be the best one to break the news to Jemma."

"Did Cindy say anything to Jemma about needing to identify Keziah?"

"No. By the time we found out her parents wouldn't do it, Jemma had already holed up in a friend's cabin. Said she wanted to be alone. Cindy said it was like Jemma built a stone wall around herself. We decided to let it go if the Taylors were able to make the identification. Which they were. I felt kinda bad afterwards, with Brenda taking it so hard."

"Tough choice."

"Yeah, but the best thing in the long run. Jemma was the one who reported Keziah missing in the first place, back in November, so she was still dealing with that. Keziah should have been in school, but Mrs. Porter supposedly called in that she was sick. Later denied making the call."

"I suppose you interviewed the parents when you learned she'd disappeared."

"If you want to call it that. We should have known how they'd react. Even the dog snarled and barked at us the whole time we were there. We made them tie it up so we could look around. All in all, about the most unproductive thirty minutes we ever spent. That is the meanest woman I ever met, and I've met some hard characters in my line of work."

"So even back then she wouldn't help."

"Nope. She said Keziah was a worthless sinner, or words to that effect, and denied that she was even their daughter. It really turned my stomach. We did take a look around. Keziah's room was pretty barren. A few schoolbooks. Nothing personal. No stuffed toys or things like that that girls usually collect."

"What about Mr. Porter. Didn't he speak up?"

"If you call mumbling 'speaking up.' He just sat there in his wheelchair and muttered something about old sins casting long shadows. Then, after Keziah'd been ID'd, Will—Sheriff Gibson—insisted we go up to the Porters' place again, whether they liked it or not. Of course it was 'or not.'"

"Poor Jemma. I guess she gets the brunt of it. That wall you say she built—isolating herself like that—it must have worried you."

"Yes and no. I didn't think she'd do something stupid. But, yeah, we worried."

"You said that Jemma and Cindy had given you the only real leads you had. I wondered if anything came of those leads—or if you can talk about them."

Tom ran one hand through his close-cropped brown hair. "I don't think it's much of a secret, but I wish it was."

"What happened?" Ryan asked.

Tom leaned back and clasped his hands behind his head. "Keziah started going out with guys she met online."

CHAPTER 21

It shouldn't have come as a surprise, but hearing it spoken out loud cut through me. "How?" I asked at last. "I mean, all kinds of questions come to mind. I thought she was pretty much under her mother's thumb. So how did she get away long enough to contact somebody online? And whose computer did she use? Jemma's?"

"You *do* ask a lot of questions."

"Occupational hazard."

Tom's smile touched his eyes. "Mine too." He looked out the window briefly, then leaned forward again. "It's hard to explain without going into all the family dynamics. Where to start.... Those people were dysfunctional to begin with, but I guess you figured that out already."

I nodded.

"Jemma's a smart kid, and she deserved a break. Graduated tops in her class. One of her teachers took her under her wing. Offered her a place to live here in town—fixed up a little 'mother-in-law' house they didn't need any more. Rent free till she could get on her feet. Then helped her find a job. She's a receptionist for a dentist. Moonlights at a restaurant a couple of nights a week."

"So she's been here about—what?—six or seven months now?"

"About that. She was all packed and ready to go on graduation day."

"I can imagine the uproar that must have caused."

"Yep. Before she left, she saw to it that Keziah had some measure of freedom, but Keziah didn't know how to handle it."

The intercom buzzed to let Tom know Jemma was here. He went to the outer office to meet her, and they both returned a minute later. A petite brunette with hair pulled back in a ponytail, she appeared quite young at first glance. But whatever the cause, her home life or dealing with the tragedy surrounding Keziah, her face bore the hard, tired lines of a much older woman. Her gray eyes were wary.

"Tom tells me you're the ones who found my sister," she said after we'd been introduced.

"Yes," Ryan said. "I wish things had been different."

Jemma nodded, giving him the slightest trace of a smile.

Tom pulled his chair from behind the desk so that he and Jemma sat facing Ryan and me. It hadn't bothered me to ask Tom questions, but with Jemma I felt I needed to do the eggshell walk.

"We've been brainstorming," Tom told her.

I didn't realize that's what we'd been doing but appreciated his diplomacy. It sure sounded better than "Sharon's been asking a lot of nosy questions."

"What did I interrupt?" Jemma asked.

"Well, I was about to explain how Keziah got access to the Internet."

Jemma bit her lip and looked at her hands, clenched tightly in her lap. "We figured she set up an account at the library, or at one of those Internet cafés." She looked at Ryan and me. "Turns out it was some kid at school."

"But...." I stopped, puzzled.

"But when did she get away from Mother Witch long enough to use it?"

"Mm. Something like that." I wasn't comfortable calling their mother names, although the one Jemma used worked for me.

Jemma looked away from us and gave a slight toss of her head, causing the ponytail to brush across her back. "Kezzie started school in Cloudcroft in fifth grade. Up through eighth grade, she toed the line. Rode the bus to school. Studied. Rode the bus home. Did chores. Listened to lectures about God's wrath."

"She never challenged that—that routine?"

"I was the rebellious one. Kezzie saw what happened when I got out of line. More chores, more tongue-lashing. No beatings—those would have shown. The last thing The Witch wanted was another visit from CYFD—or from any other agency. I told her she'd better take care of Dad too, not that he deserved it, or someone would be down on her like flies in July."

The steel in Jemma's voice chilled me. I wondered if it was her iron will that had kept her from breaking under the cruelty and if Keziah had been too breakable to stand up under it.

"I thought Kezzie would be okay when I moved away," Jemma continued, facing us again. "I talked to one of the counselors at school, and she actually visited our house, even though it was summer and school had already let out. She told our parents they *had* to let Kezzie have some outside activities. I don't know if she really had that clout or not, but the threat of 'government interference' was the only thing that ever scared them."

"Was that when Keziah started going to the Teen Center?" Ryan asked.

Jemma nodded. "And that was a good thing. If she'd just stuck to that. The Nelsons, the people who got me out of hell, let me use one of their cars whenever I wanted. I told Kezzie I'd see that she got home from the Center. And she could always come to my place."

"But something changed," I murmured.

"She met some boy when school started last fall. That's when she started lying. I never thought she'd lie to *me*."

There was a flicker of anguish in Jemma's eyes—the first crack I'd seen in her carefully constructed mask.

CHAPTER 22

"When I found out Kezzie had lied, I felt so—so *betrayed*," Jemma said. "I lashed out at her. Then I saw that 'shut-down' look in her face. I told her right away that I was sorry, that I didn't mean to sound like The Witch. She said it was okay, but I knew it wasn't."

"Did it ever come up again, the lying I mean?" I asked.

"No, we just acted as if everything was the same. I'd still give her rides when she needed them. And she stayed over sometimes. But all we talked about were things that didn't matter."

"Did you ever get the feeling she'd *like* to confide in you again?"

Jemma thought that over. "No, *I* was the one who felt guilty. For saying things I couldn't undo. If she felt guilty—about lying or anything else—it sure didn't show."

"If it's any help, it sounds to me as if she'd already made up her mind about something. I don't think there's anything you could have said, or any other way you could have said it, that would change that."

Jemma stared at me a moment, then shrugged. "I'll have to think about that." She stood to go. "Well, it's been nice meeting you two, but I have to get back to work."

* * *

"I feel like I cracked a few of those eggs I'd tried not walking on," I told Ryan after Tom left the room to see Jemma off. "I must have stepped on some nerve for her to leave so abruptly."

"Take your own advice, honey. I don't think you said anything that caused her to leave. She had to go to work. That's all."

When Tom returned, he took a seat across from us again. "I'm glad you met Jemma yourselves. Less explaining for me to do."

"This boy that Keziah lied about," Ryan said. "Was this the guy she met online?"

"No. He's the one who bragged about what a computer genius he is. We talked to him not long after Keziah went missing. Scared him, uh, spitless."

"So all he did was show Keziah how to get online?"

"That's about it. They'd go over to his house and work on his computer. His mother thought it was nice they were getting so much homework done." Tom rolled his eyes. "Well, he made straight A's, so I guess that made sense to her."

"No romantic stuff?" I asked.

"Not between the two of them. This kid—Joel—seemed more interested in showing her how smart he was. He helped her set up an email account. Set her up with three to be exact. Plus a networking site."

"Did he know she was using email to meet other guys?"

"Yeah, but he claimed he thought it was just a game with her, that she didn't plan to follow through."

"It didn't bother him?"

"Joel's not interested in girls. No jealousy. No strings. Maybe that's what made their relationship work."

"Okay, Here's what I'm piecing together," I said. "Tell me if I'm off track. Here's this fourteen-year-old girl who's been repressed all her life discovering she's a sexual being. She and Joel aren't attracted to each other, but strangers she meets online give her the kind of attention she's never had."

"Are you a psychologist too?"

"Just the armchair kind."

"Did you find out who those guys were?" Ryan asked.

"One of them. Someone at the base. He said they actually got together at some dive on the edge of town. But when he found out she was 'jail bait,' as he put it, he got out of there."

"Do you believe him?"

Tom made a slight back-and-forth gesture with his hand. "He's still on the radar."

"I take it you haven't had any luck tracking down anyone else," I said.

"There were several guys who responded to the site she set up, but only three she replied to. The one we talked to, and two others. They were a little cagier. Used fake IDs to set up accounts at one of those places that offers free Internet access. So far we've drawn a blank."

"I've hesitated to tell you this because it sounds so off-the-wall," I said, changing the subject, "but I'd like to toss it out there and see what you think."

Between the two of us, Ryan and I related the conversation we'd overheard at Ernie's. It sounded even more far-fetched in the re-telling, but Tom listened intently.

"I went so far as to look up sex offenders in this area," I said, "and I did find someone who looked like the man we called Mr. Nondescript. His name is Horace Waller. He goes by Bulldog."

"We know about Bulldog. And it's quite possible you did see him. His looks are misleading. Mr. Nice Guy outside, but sly and arrogant inside. I think he likes to thumb his nose at the cops, walking just to the edge of the line, but careful not to cross it."

"I wonder if the cowboy reported it."

"Could be. Every now and then someone calls the local cops to say they've seen him around town—here, Cloudcroft, Ruidoso, Tulie, somewhere else. Whether it's their imagination or if they've really seen him or someone who looks like him, it's hard to tell."

"And not much you can do about it."

"It's nice to talk to someone who knows something about law enforcement. It's hard to convince some people that we can't arrest a person just because we don't like his looks. Not yet, anyway."

"So all these people who might or might not be Bulldog are so law-abiding they don't even jaywalk," Ryan said.

"That's about the size of it. We do check out the sightings, if possible, and we do keep an eye on Bulldog and his fellow sleazes as best we can. We have to walk a thin line not to violate their rights."

"I'm guessing you know what kind of car he drives—license number and all that?" I asked.

"We try to stay ahead of him. He frequents the used-car lots, mostly in El Paso, makes a trade-in, pays cash for some bucket of bolts the dealer is probably glad to get rid of."

"I'm curious about his latest. Our friend's aunt claims she followed him to El Paso. Long unreliable story from unreliable source. Still, *someone* caused her to wreck her car, and it seems likely it was the person she was following. Bulldog or someone else."

"Did she report it?"

"Someone did." I told Tom about our fruitless search for any helpful details. "I know this won't prove anything, but would you mind telling me about Bulldog's current car?"

"No problem." Tom took a seat behind the desk again and turned to the computer. With a few keystrokes, he had the latest info on Bulldog.

I felt oddly disappointed that his car had New Mexico plates. "The car Alvina followed had California plates."

"That's what you're looking for? Well, there could be a connection after all. But it's a long shot."

"I'll take it."

"Bulldog has an aunt from California who visits from time to time. We know he borrows her car, but figure he thinks it's a smart move on his part, so we just let him go on thinking he's smart. It's kind of a cat-and-mouse game, each of us trying to out-think the other."

"Do you know if he was driving it Saturday?"

Tom looked at the computer screen again and shook his head. "I wish I could tell you. He drove it Friday. Too much action on a Saturday night to keep tabs on Bulldog. Hmm. If he was driving his aunt's car, and it was involved in that accident, I bet she was a little pissed. Even if it was just a fender-bender on his part."

"And even if the accident was unavoidable, even if it wasn't his fault, it might take the wind out of his sails," Ryan said.

"You're right," I added. "Sneaky's one thing, being in the spotlight something else."

"We'll keep an eye out," Tom said. "See if he's driving a damaged 'California' car. Can't do anything about it unless there's a direct connection between that car and your friend's accident."

Oh, that fourth amendment. "Stonewalled," I said.

"For now. There's always hope. He can't go on forever without slipping up."

CHAPTER 23

I wished I'd taken up knitting so I could be doing something inconspicuous while waiting for Dot to arrive at the Teen Center. Rather, while hoping she'd show.

On the other hand, I enjoyed sitting with Brenda and hearing more about the upcoming musical.

"The girl who plays Laurey has already learned her lines and knows all the songs. She has a beautiful voice," Brenda said, as the knitting needles clicked rhythmically in her skillful fingers.

"Where will they perform?"

"Believe it or not, they're constructing a stage in the shop. One of the churches graciously offered to let them use their parish hall, but it seemed simpler to build it here rather than haul sets back and forth."

"Ryan enjoys helping out. In fact, he's over there this afternoon."

"It works both ways. Darryl is glad for his company, as well as the extra help."

"What will they do with all the woodworking stuff when rehearsals start? Move everything against the walls?"

"Right. And several of the churches are lending folding chairs for the performance. So things are falling into place. Now if only Curly would learn *his* lines."

I'm convinced there's a magnetic force that draws you toward someone who's watching you. I looked across the room to see Dot, arms folded across her chest, standing by the door. She was wearing a parka and snow boots, so I gathered she'd just come inside.

I smiled at her and waggled my fingers a tad. Just enough of a wave to let her know I'd seen her. She lifted her chin in what I hoped was a nod and an invitation to join her. Then she turned and went back outside again. I excused myself and followed her to the parking lot.

The cold bit into my face. I snugged the hood of my parka, then dug my hands into my pockets, wishing I'd thought to bring gloves. The wind whipped Dot's hair, but she seemed oblivious. Maybe people who grew up in this climate didn't even notice.

We stood face to face without speaking, and I wondered if I'd misinterpreted her gesture to meet with her. She bent down, unzipped the side of one of her boots, unrolled the top of her sock, and pulled out a clove cigarette along with a small flat lighter. She rezipped her boot, straightened up, lit the cigarette, and slipped the lighter into her pocket. Then she turned slightly so the smoke wouldn't blow in my face.

"Is there someplace we could go get some hot chocolate?" I asked.

She shrugged. "Happy's, I guess."

At least she seemed to take my suggestion in stride, however unenthusiastically. Better than asking if I was out of my mind.

"My car's parked over there," I said, pulling my gloveless hand out of my pocket and waving toward a row of cars nearby. *And it has a heater.*

She trudged after me, and I pretended we were walking side by side.

"I hate to ask you not to smoke in the car," I said over my shoulder, "but it's not ours...."

She shrugged again, dropped the cigarette to the asphalt, smashed it out with the toe of her boot, then caught up with me. "Otherwise you'd be delighted."

I laughed. "Otherwise I wouldn't care."

The eye that wasn't hidden under the platinum mop registered surprise. "You don't care if I get cancer?"

"Dot, you have the makings of a lawyer. Of course I don't want you to get cancer. But I don't want to run your life either."

We got in the car, and I started the engine.

"I suppose you want me to buckle up too," she said.

"Yeah, I wish you would."

"Just because it's not your car."

"Pick any law school you'd like, Dot, and I'll send a written recommendation."

She grimaced and buckled up. "With my grades, I'll be lucky to get out of high school."

I pulled out onto the street. "It can be a drag."

"I bet you sailed through school with straight A's."

"Only my senior year. I nearly flunked out my junior year."

"Huh!" She stared out the window, probably hoping against a "just-look-at-me-now" lecture, which I wouldn't have dumped on her anyway.

She directed me to Happy's Convenience Store, where we each got hot cocoa from a machine. There were two unoccupied booths next to the windows, so we picked one, seated ourselves across from each other, and shed our coats.

I supposed this was as private a place as any, since most customers probably came for milk or bread—some item they'd forgotten to pick up at the grocery story—and not for fine dining.

We sipped our cocoa for a minute or two before Dot broke the silence.

"When you found Kezzie," she said, "what did she look like? Was it horrible?"

I hadn't expected the question and took a few moments to choose my words. "The *situation* was upsetting. But the way Keziah looked wasn't upsetting. She was all bundled up in winter clothes—"

"You're sure?" Dot interrupted. "I was afraid she might be, you know, just partway dressed."

"No. She was fully dressed. Except for the circumstances, she looked quite normal—almost as if she'd simply lain down to rest."

Dot let out a long breath and rubbed her eye as if she was afraid I might notice her trying not to cry. I handed her a paper napkin from the dispenser, then turned my attention to my cooling cocoa. Dot pushed her hair away from her face, her hand trembling, and blotted both eyes. I resisted the temptation to go sit beside her and hold her in my arms so she could cry the pain out.

"Do they know what happened?" she asked, trying to sound nonchalant.

"Not that I've heard. I've been trying to figure it out myself. If she went up the mountain to ski, maybe she fell down and couldn't get up."

"No way," Dot scoffed. "She'd know how to get up. Those girls—Kezzie and her sister—could ski before they could walk. Because of where they lived. It was the only way they could get out sometimes."

"Well, the way I look at it, there're lots of possibilities. She went up there to be alone, to think something out. She went expecting to meet someone. Someone who never showed up. She went *with* someone. He left her there for some reason and told her he'd come back. Maybe he meant to come back but got lost. Or...maybe he never meant to come back."

Dot tightened her jaw and crumpled the napkin in her hand. "The bastard!"

I nodded in agreement, unsure about voicing my questions. *Who? Who left her there to die?* I screamed silently.

CHAPTER 24

"Can you talk about it?" I asked softly.

Dot bristled, then relented. "At first we kind of envied her, going behind her mother's back and getting away with it. But then she got, like, way overboard."

"Behind her mother's back. That must have taken some doing."

"*Oh* yeah. She swiped some letterhead paper from the counselor's office and got Joel to type something up, something about some night classes she had to take to bring up her grades. Joel's real smart and he could make it sound like a grown-up had written it."

"And her mother fell for it."

"Shee-it. My mother would have marched down to the school and raised hell. But I guess Mrs. Porter had some history with the school board and CYFD and I don't know what all. So she stayed away. And Kezzie was kinda cagey too. She made it for just one night a week, not every night."

"That's pretty inventive."

"Yeah, we thought—me and Wilma and Phyllis—we thought she was just makin' out with ol' Joel. He's kinda nerdy, but—" She shrugged and pushed her hair out of her face. "At least he's her age."

"Hmm."

"Joel's had a crush on Kezzie for-EV-er."

That didn't jibe with what Tom had told us, but I didn't want to question it. Now that she'd gotten started, Dot seemed relieved to have someone to tell, and the words kept tumbling out.

"But Kezzie was just using him to find guys online," Dot said. "I mean, I don't think she was that blunt. Maybe Joel didn't know she was meeting them."

"The other guys." *Who were they? How many?*

"She started bragging about it to me and Phyllis and Wilma. At first we thought it was kinda cool, and then—I don't know—it just didn't feel right."

"I think you have good intuition."

Dot nodded vigorously, and the blonde curtain fell over her eye again. She pushed it away and looked at me intently. "That was what bothered us about Kezzie. She was, like, so clueless. And she wouldn't listen to us."

"So you tried to discourage her?"

"A little. We didn't want to sound bossy like her mother. Maybe we should have tried harder." Dot's shoulders sagged, and tears threatened again.

"Don't blame yourself. Sometimes people just aren't ready to listen."

"We never thought...."

"I saw the posters," I said, changing the subject. "Did her mother put them up?"

"Oh, right. Like *she'd* care. Jemma put them up. But she didn't even know till about a week later."

"Really?"

"Yeah." Dot looked down, and clenched her jaw. Her hair drooped over one eye again.

My heart sank. I hoped she hadn't decided she'd said enough.

"Would you like some more hot chocolate? Mine has gotten cold."

She didn't object, so I chose to take that as a "yes." I stood and picked up our cups, got refills from the machine, then returned to our booth.

"I probably talk too much," she mumbled.

I stirred my cocoa, wishing I could add a big fat marshmallow, wishing I knew what to say. "It has to be hard to talk about," I ventured.

She didn't answer.

Well, here goes. "It sounds like Jemma didn't know what was going on."

Dot sat up straighter. "No, Kezzie quit telling her things after she started going out with those guys on the base."

"It sounds like there were lots of guys."

"Nah. Not that many. I think a couple of them dropped her after they found out how young she was. But there was one—"

"One she kept seeing."

"She made us promise not to tell. I don't guess it matters now. She said they were in love and she was going to run away with him. We tried to talk her into waiting. But in a way we couldn't blame her, the way everything was so miserable at home. She told us they were leaving the next day for California, and we weren't supposed to tell a soul."

I felt my stomach turn over. They were children after all, no matter how grown up fourteen-year-olds thought they were. "You really were put on the spot."

"When the cops started asking questions, Phyllis thought we should say something, but me and Wilma talked her out of it. We really didn't know anything. Who the guy was. Where they were going. We figured the cops would just get mad at us and ask us more questions. Like we knew more than we did."

"You're right. You couldn't have added anything. But now that she's been found, they'll probably ask questions again. But I don't think they'll get mad."

"Ms. T. says you're a lawyer. If they do get mad, can we call you?"

I smiled and dared to reach over and hold her hand. "I am, and you can."

CHAPTER 25

Alvina accosted me on my way to the cocktail gathering for the symposium participants. She had talked Mela into letting her go to Rebecca's for dinner, insisting she was suffering from cabin fever. Mela, probably feeling a little shut in herself, browsed in the gift shop while Alvina and I talked.

"They say my car is totaled, which doesn't mean it's beyond repair. It's just what the insurance people say when they'd rather pay to replace it than have it fixed. So I'm going down to El Paso to see for myself."

"That's a good idea."

"Don't patronize me."

I didn't bother to answer, just made a point of looking at my watch.

"While I'm there," she continued, "I'm going to find out if the car that hit me has been brought somewhere for repairs."

Good luck on that one.

"I telephoned that incompetent sheriff in Alamogordo today, and he wasn't any help at all. So I'm going to have the El Paso cops put out an APB on a California car with a damaged front end."

Lucky cops. "By the way, how soon are you leaving?"

"Tomorrow morning."

"So you'll be staying with Mela for a while?"

"A day or two. I don't want to spend my whole vacation in El Paso."

It occurred to me that I had no idea where Alvina lived, or what she was vacating *from*, so I asked.

"Not that it's any of your business, but I work for a collections agency in Austin."

"How many vacation days do you have left?"

"You sure are nosy, missy."

"That's what I do for a living. Ask nosy questions. Sometimes I forget I'm on vacation."

"So how many vacation days do *you* have left?"

"We'll leave about a week from now—next Wednesday or Thursday. It's going by fast. Which reminds me, I'm here for a conference of nosy people, and I need to join them for cocktails."

* * *

The symposium was off to a good start. I met a number of congenial souls, and only one obnoxious person, which, percentagewise, was an optimistic sign.

Following Wednesday morning's seminar, I got together with my fellow panelists to coordinate our presentation. After that, we were free until later in the day.

A history buff, Ryan had found a number of books about Cloudcroft's earlier days. And even though this wasn't the Taylors' day to volunteer at the Teen Center, Ryan had gotten so involved in building the set for the musical that he planned to go there later this afternoon.

I had told Dot that I'd talk with Tom Alderete and was glad his schedule coincided with mine. The drive into Alamogordo seemed shorter each time, and I arrived at 1:00, fifteen minutes before our appointment.

Sheriff Gibson was in his office, hunched over his desk, sorting through a pile of paperwork. I knocked lightly at his door. A wide grin spread across his otherwise somber face as he looked up to greet me. He stood and ushered me into his office.

"I can only stay a minute," I said. I started to wave away his suggestion to sit down, but knew he'd remain standing until I sat. So I settled myself on the dark-blue chair facing him.

"Ms. Piffle told me she'd called to give you some advice," I said.

Sheriff Gibson sat down again, leaned back in his chair and drummed his fingers on the armrests. He gave me a woeful look, till he saw the laughter in my eyes.

He shook his head, a glint of humor in his own eyes. "You could say that," he drawled. "We did take down her complaint, for the record."

"I'm glad," I said. "Just in case anything comes of it. I know there's nothing concrete to go on, but I think she might have seen Bulldog. And I think it's possible he caused her car accident."

Sheriff Gibson raised his eyebrows. "Hearing it from you—in a coherent form—well, that does give it a little credence. It's still pretty nebulous."

"I know. But—another occupational hazard—sometimes I find myself playing devil's advocate."

He smiled. "That's not a bad thing."

I rose to leave. "I'm supposed to meet Tom Alderete in a few minutes, so I'd better be on my way."

"Stop by anytime. A dose of common sense in my business is always welcome."

CHAPTER 26

The door to Tom's office was open, and he waved me in. Like Sheriff Gibson, he had a sizable stack of paperwork on his desk.

"I don't want to take up too much of your time," I said as I sat opposite him. "But I do need to talk with you. It's easier in person than on the phone."

"You don't need to apologize. I'm always glad for an excuse to procrastinate. Coffee?"

"No thanks. I'm pretty coffee'd out from the meetings this morning."

"Oh, that's right. The symposium. How's it going so far?"

"So far, so good."

"Glad to hear it. I know Janet worked pretty hard to put it all together." He paused. "So tell me, what's on your mind?"

"Well, I talked with Keziah's friend Dot yesterday. I don't even know her last name."

"Blanchard. Dorothy Blanchard." A mixture of surprise and curiosity showed in Tom's face, but he waited for me to continue.

"I know you batted out the first time someone tried to interview Dot and her friends," I said. "They simply weren't ready then. But I think they'd be willing to come forward now."

Tom picked up a pen on his desk and rolled it between his hands. "You must think they have something helpful to say."

"I'm not sure," I admitted. "Dot did say a couple of things that didn't jibe with what I'd heard from you. But I think you'd have a better handle on how to sort the wheat from the chaff." I cleared my throat. "I need to tell you...Dot would like me to be present."

Tom quit twirling his pen and raised one eyebrow. "Not surprising. Evidently she trusts you. And believe me, I'm all for it."

"Just so there's not any misunderstanding, she wants me to act as her lawyer. Not that she needs one," I hastened to add. "I'm not even licensed to practice in New Mexico. But it seemed to ease her mind that I'd be there with her. I don't know if she's seen too many TV shows with suspects being closed up in tiny cells while the cops yell at them and push them around."

Tom sighed and ran his hand over his crew cut. "That's why we talked to them at their homes. With their parents hanging around in the background."

"Do you think the parents might have put a crimp in things?"

"I didn't get that feeling. No, especially since we got the same story—rather *non*-story—from each of them. They'd decided ahead of time what they wouldn't say. Will tried to get across that Keziah could be in danger, but they just said, in so many words, they were sorry they couldn't help. Of course we didn't believe them, but short of getting out those rubber hoses...."

I laughed. "Oh, right. What I'm wondering, even though their stories matched, was there any difference in their individual demeanor, their body language?"

"Definitely. There was one I thought would tell us something, one that got a little teary-eyed. But in the end, she stuck to her story."

"Phyllis," I murmured.

He nodded. "Now Dot changing her mind, that's a real turnaround."

"What she's really afraid of is that you all are mad at them for waiting so long."

"She might have something there."

"I don't blame you. But try to keep it in check. No rubber hoses."

Tom grinned. "Okay, boss. Now. Let's set up a date and time we can all get together before she changes her mind again." He turned to the calendar on his computer. "When will you be free?" he asked as he made a few keystrokes.

"Any afternoon after today. That should work for Dot too." I hesitated. "Do we necessarily have to meet at her house? I mean, if there's someplace else she'd be more comfortable, would that work as well?"

He thought a few moments, then faced me again. "I don't see why not. As long as there's another adult present. Meaning, you, if that's okay with her parents. Do you have her phone number?"

I nodded.

"Why don't you see if she can meet with us tomorrow?"

I looked at my watch. "Tell you what. I'll drive by the Teen Center on my way back, and see if she's there. I'd rather ask her in person. I can get a better feel for her response that way. I'll call you back as soon as I know something."

CHAPTER 27

After my visit with Tom, I sped back to Cloudcroft as fast as the curvy road would allow. I slowed down at the Village limit and drove straight to the shop adjoinng the Teen Center. There I stopped long enough to see Ryan. He assured me he'd find a ride back to The Lodge with one of the volunteers.

Next I zipped into the Teen Center and waved at Stephania, who was on duty for the day. I found Dot, Wilma, and Phyllis in their usual spot, this time playing a game of Clue.

"I'm sorry to interrupt," I said, "but I need to talk with Dot a minute, and I have to be someplace else pretty soon. Dot can tell you all about it later."

"It's about talking to the sheriff, isn't it," Wilma said, studying me through her Coke-bottle lenses.

"Yes, it is."

"Does he want to talk to all of us?"

"Maybe. Probably. Now that things are changed."

"Now that Kezzie's dead, you mean."

"Yes."

"Quit bugging her," Dot said, rising languidly and moving away from their table. "She said she was in a hurry, so y'all can ask her questions later."

"It's really not all that secret," I said as we walked toward the vending machine, "but it might be easier to discuss by ourselves."

Dot put some coins in the machine and pulled out a bottle of orange juice. "So?"

"If you're not busy tomorrow after school, we can meet with Sgt. Alderete then."

Dot gave me a considering look. "Okay."

"Good. I'll let him know. Now, where would you like to meet? Here? At your house? Someplace else?"

"Hmph. I just supposed we'd go to his office."

"That's fine by me. Is that what you'd like to do?"

She took a swig of her juice. "Yeah."

"Make sure it's okay with your mom and call me back. If I don't answer, leave a message. Sorry to sound so rushed, but I'm supposed to be in a meeting and I might have my phone turned off."

She shrugged and brushed her hair out of her face. "Mom won't mind."

"Best to let her know anyway. I'll call you back as soon as I can." I gave her a bright smile and a pat on the arm before hurrying on my way.

I gave Tom a quick call to tell him to expect Dot and me "sometime" tomorrow, and I'd fill him in later. By then, I had about ten minutes to get to the symposium.

Dot, don't change your mind, I prayed as I drove up the hill. *Dot's mother, please say yes.*

* * *

After spending the day rushing here and there, then getting caught up in stimulating discussions at the symposium, I was ready for a change of pace.

In fact, I could hardly wait to spend some time with Ryan. We unwound with a glass of wine in the lounge before dining at Rebecca's. Over dinner we exchanged tales of our day. I had described Keziah's friends earlier and had explained my need to contact Tom.

"So Miss Dot is ready to tell all," he said.

"I hope so." Though it was tempting to share Dot's version of Keziah's disappearance with Ryan, I didn't want to break her confidence. Just as I hadn't wanted to give the details to Tom.

Right after dinner, I finally reached Dot.

"Guess what!" she said.

"Tell me."

"Wilma and Phyllis and Joel want to go down there and talk to Sgt. Alderete too. If you have room for all of us."

Gulp. "I have no objections. But keep in mind that he'll want to talk with you one at a time rather than all together. By the way, I'll need written permission from all the parents. That it's okay to ride with me, when, where, why."

"Both parents?"

"No. One'll do. One per kid."

"Phyllis's mom probably won't let her go."

"Up to her. The visit to the sheriff isn't compulsory. Permission is."

I held my breath, expecting some static, but instead she asked if I'd be the lawyer for all of them. "We'll pay you."

"Don't worry. Sometimes I do things pro bono. Now, let me see. First things first. Let me check with Sgt. Alderete and make sure he has enough time for everyone. I'll call you as soon as I hear from him, okay?"

"Sure."

I rang off and called the sheriff's office, hoping someone might have night duty. As it turned out, Sheriff Gibson was still there, still trying to catch up on his paperwork. I explained the latest developments concerning Dot and her friends.

"Obviously, this isn't an emergency," I said. "But I didn't know how soon Tom would be coming in tomorrow, and I need to connect with him before getting back to the girls."

"He should be here at 8:00. Will that be soon enough?"

I hesitated. "Sure. If you'd leave him a note to call me first thing, I'd appreciate it."

"You bet."

Sometimes I think I ought to have a phone embedded in my brain. End one call; start another. I phoned Dot next. She didn't answer, so I left the same message I'd been leaving all day: "Call me."

Two minutes later, Tom called. Whether Sheriff Gibson had heard the hesitation in my voice, or whether he liked the fact that I wasn't demanding, I don't know. But he had relayed my message to Tom right away instead of waiting till tomorrow morning.

"Well," Tom said, after I'd explained the situation, "it's the old 'good news, bad news' story. Good news, I have time and I won't have to track them down. Bad news—maybe—I wonder if they've concocted some fairy-tale together."

"Could be, but Dot was pretty straightforward when she talked to me. Besides, this time it was *their* idea, and I think they'd really like to help."

"Let's give it a try. Will 4:00 work?"

I assured him it would, and we ironed out a few details before hanging up.

I left another message for Dot: "I need to pick you up by 3:15 tomorrow. Let me know where."

A minute later she called back. "Phyllis's mother wants to tag along." I could tell by the edge in her voice how Dot felt about the tagalong.

"So she can drive if you don't have room for all of us," she added.

"That'll help."

We arranged to meet at the school, and *finally* I got off the phone for the night and turned my thoughts to tomorrow's symposium.

CHAPTER 28

From early Thursday morning through early afternoon, the symposium featured panel discussions, including my own. Ryan had gone to all the sessions, first as a favor to me and later because they piqued his interest

"Not that I'm biased," he told me when the meetings ended for the day, "but I thought your panel was the most thought-provoking. And of course, your part shone. I liked the way you put a face on immigrants."

"You *are* biased, but I thank you anyway."

We rehashed parts of the program till it was time to get ready for the kids' appointment with Tom.

"I'm glad the symposium went so well," I said. "I have no idea what to expect this afternoon. I wish you'd come with us."

"You need my moral support for this too?" he teased.

"Always!"

* * *

Despite Dot's misgivings, I welcomed Charlene Wood, Phyllis's mother, when we gathered to carpool to Alamogordo. I figured if the other parents discussed the trip among themselves, they were probably happier knowing Charlene was chaperoning, rather than letting their children go traipsing off with a complete stranger.

Charlene, a trim redhead with shoulder-length hair and brown eyes, was friendly and chipper, but I sensed an underlying nervousness. Phyllis was somewhat glum, since the other kids had elected to ride with Ryan and me.

"We can trade around on the way back," I suggested. "It's a short trip anyway." I'd thought of suggesting that Wilma or Joel ride with the Woods, but had a couple of reasons for re-thinking that idea.

First of all, I could be sure none of my passengers discussed whatever they'd decided to tell Tom. Just in case they'd already collaborated, there'd be no rehearsals. And second, I was frankly curious to see how they interacted.

Ryan opened the back door for our group, and Joel scuttled in ahead of the girls.

"Hey, scoot over, Joel," Dot said as she climbed into the back seat. "Haven't you ever heard of 'ladies first'?"

"Joel's not into etiquette," Wilma said as she followed Dot.

"I have to sit by the window," Joel whined.

"Sheesh, what a baby," Dot said.

She turned her attention to Ryan as she fastened her seatbelt. "So, Mr. Salazar. Ms. Taylor tells me you teach school in Texas. How come you're here instead of in school?"

Ryan looked back at Dot and smiled. "We start early in August, then have a long winter break."

"Wow. I wish we did that. Well, not start early, just had long breaks. Tomorrow's our last day of school till next year."

Ryan started the engine and pulled out of the parking lot, his eyes on the road ahead. "What are you all going to do with your free time?"

"We're going to spend Christmas with my grandparents in Phoenix," Joel said. "Bo-o-ring."

"We're going to Taos for a whole day to ski. My parents say it's too expensive to stay longer. Especially with Sierra

Blanca in our back yard." Dot heaved a drama-filled sigh. "Oh well, Sierra Blanca's fun too."

I found myself analyzing the group dynamics. Despite wanting to keep an open mind, I'd have to look hard to find something to like about Joel. It might help if his personality didn't match his face, I decided. A long pointy nose and small close-set eyes made me think of a weasel, or at best a recently sharpened pencil.

Dot was uncharacteristically chatty and personable. I chalked it up to excitement over the holidays ahead.

Or possibly over Ryan's presence. I'd noticed the slight flirtatious note in her voice, and when I glanced back I saw that she'd pushed her hair out of her face. I smiled to myself. She seemed more like a normal teen-ager than when we'd first met.

Wilma was an enigma. She hadn't added anything to the conversation about their vacation, and I'd picked up mixed messages from our earlier meetings. Withdrawn at times, prickly at others.

"So. Have you met Rebecca?" Dot asked.

I hesitated a beat. "No-o. I've heard she only visits non-believers. So she probably won't visit me." *And if that's true, who sent that psychic warning a few days ago?*

"What about you, Mr. Salazar? Are you a believer?"

Ryan chuckled. "I'm an undecider."

"Jemma says she saw her."

My ears perked up. "Jemma?"

"Yeah. She works at The Lodge sometimes when they're extra busy. In Housekeeping."

"Hmm. Tell us when she saw Rebecca."

"I don't know exactly. Last year? She said Rebecca threw a salt shaker at her. Well, not *at* her. Rebecca was just kidding around. She doesn't try to hurt people, just scare them a little. The salt shaker, like, bounced off the wall and didn't even break. Jemma said she thought it was kinda funny, so Rebecca winked at her and disappeared."

"Now I wish I was an unbeliever. I'd like to see that lady in action!"

"Jemma's a liar," Joel scoffed.

"Shut up, Joel," Dot said.

All three settled into silence. As we neared Alamogordo, I think they'd begun to give serious thought to the reason for our trip. If they'd compared notes earlier, they certainly didn't give any sign of it now.

CHAPTER 29

Tom's greeting set the tone for the interviews: pleasant but without a forced heartiness. He shook hands with each of us, smiling at Charlene and telling her it was nice to see her again.

"I really appreciate you kids volunteering to come down to Alamo," he said. He turned to Charlene and smiled at her again. "And I appreciate your volunteering to carpool. I doubt that any of the parents need to be present, but I recruited Ms. Salazar to be an advocate for the kids if they ask."

Wow. That was smooth, if only partly truthful. It was Dot's "recruiting," not his, that won me this role. Charlene looked a little befuddled, since I'm sure she'd planned to sit in on Phyllis's interview.

There was no subtle way to tell her to butt out, that parents sometimes throw a monkey wrench into the proceedings. But after Tom's diplomatic explanation, I suppose she realized it would be awkward for her to insist on accompanying her daughter.

"Since it was Dot's idea to get everyone together," Tom said. "I'll interview her first. I know the waiting area is small, but I hope you'll make yourselves comfortable while waiting your turn. It shouldn't take long."

Those remaining all sat down, Charlene and the kids looking somewhat ill-at-ease. Ryan was the only one who seemed relaxed. He has a knack for interacting with teenagers (one of many qualities that make him a good teacher). So I trusted he could lighten their anxiety and that Charlene would join in.

Dot and I followed Tom into his office and seated ourselves across from him. Dot, hair drooped over one eye again and arms folded across her chest, bore an expression that read, "Let the torture begin."

Tom, an expert in body language I'm sure, spoke gently. "Thanks again for coming in, Dot. This is just an informal meeting. I'm not even going to record it, unless something comes up that you think should be put on tape. That okay?"

Her tension lessened, though it didn't disappear entirely.

"Sharon hasn't told me anything, except that you have new information. We can start wherever you'd like, or maybe at the end rather than the beginning."

When she didn't respond, he said, "Okay. For openers, would you happen to know why Keziah was on Ventosa Peak?"

"No." Dot unfolded her arms and twisted her hands together in her lap. "Well, we came up with some ideas. Rather, Ms. Salazar did." She looked at me, and I nodded encouragingly.

"I think she went up there to meet someone," she said. "Or maybe they went up there together. And he left her!" Indignation flashed across her face.

"That sounds logical. Do you have any idea who it might have been?"

"Maybe. Probably the one she was going to run away with."

"Want to tell me about that?"

After a somewhat fumbling start, Dot told Tom essentially the same thing she'd told me: how Joel had helped Keziah set up email accounts, how the girls had thought she was pretty brave at first but had become worried as time went by, how Keziah had sworn them to secrecy about her plan to run away.

"We tried to talk her out of it. I guess we didn't try hard enough." A tear slid down her face, and she reached for a Kleenex from the box Tom had thoughtfully placed near the edge of the desk.

"It's not your fault."

"Maybe it is," she said under her breath.

"What makes you say that?"

Dot's face turned pink as she looked away from us. "She—I quit listening to her."

"That happens."

"You don't understand." Dot choked back a sob. "I should have listened!"

Tom was quiet a while, giving her time to collect herself.

"You know how I told you we kind of admired her at first? Well, after a while, I thought she was just showing off, that she'd never met any of those guys she talked about. And I just got, like—irritated."

Tom nodded. "I might have thought that too. That she was exaggerating. And she might have been."

"But she wasn't! Don't you see? There really was someone, and if I'd listened I might have found out something about him." Dot yanked out another tissue, taking her frustration out on the Kleenex box.

"Maybe the other girls remember something you didn't. And maybe you remembered something they didn't. It'll all come together."

She digested this and even managed a small smile.

"Anything else you'd like to tell me?" Tom asked.

"I can't think of anything." She turned to me again. "Did I leave anything out?"

"You did fine. I'm not sure if it's important, but you might tell Sgt. Alderete why Joel was willing to help Keziah, and also where you think she and her boyfriend were going."

"Oh, that's right. Kezzie *said* they were going to California, but obviously they didn't."

"You sure?" Tom asked.

Dot's eye widened as she sorted out the timeline. "Well, I guess they could have gone there and come back. I mean, well, I don't know how long it was before she was found." She swallowed hard. "Was she up there a long time?"

"No. We don't know all the details yet, but—no, it was less than a day."

"Oh, I'm glad of that." Dot paused. "About Joel—" She brushed her hair back and rolled her eyes. "He was in love with her. Not that he'll let on when you talk to him. Sheesh. He's a jerk, but I didn't think it was right for Kezzie to take him for a ride like that."

I admired Tom's ability to keep a poker face. It's not one of my talents, but since I was expecting Dot to reveal Joel's feelings for Keziah, something Tom hadn't known before, I managed to look blank.

"Well, thank you, Dot," Tom said. "I appreciate your help. That should be all, unless you think of something else. If you do, just give me a call."

I couldn't tell if Dot was relieved or disappointed that the interview was so matter-of-fact and non-threatening. We joined the others in the waiting room, and Tom asked Wilma to take her turn. She asked if I'd come in with her, so I suspected she wasn't as blasé as she'd like to appear.

CHAPTER 30

Tom began the interview with Wilma much the same as he'd done with Dot. When he asked if she knew what Keziah was doing on Ventosa Peak, she just looked down at her hands and shook her head. This caused her glasses to slip down her nose, and she shoved them back in a swift practiced motion.

"Do you think she was meeting somebody special up there?"

She shook her head again.

"Dot told me that Keziah met some guys online and that you all agreed not to tell anyone," Tom said softly. "So I understand why you didn't say anything at the time. But it might help us to know now."

"Did he kill her?"

"It's possible he had something to do with her death, but until we get the autopsy report, we won't know exactly how she died. In any case, we'd like to question the guy she planned to meet."

"She didn't tell us his last name, but she called him Frank. Would that help?"

"It might. Yes, I think so."

"Joel might know. He probably looked at all her emails."

Tom's poker face cracked a bit as he raised an eyebrow. "Do you think it bothered Joel?"

"That she was using him to meet other guys?" She shrugged. "You'll have to ask him."

"I will. But I wondered about your impression."

"In case he won't answer?"

Tom grinned in spite of himself. "I won't hold you to it if the answers don't match. I'm just trying to get the picture."

"I think Joel thought if he did all these nice things for Kezzie, she'd like him."

"I see. About this Frank. Did she say anything else about him? Describe him?"

Wilma looked up at the ceiling and spoke in a breathless high-pitched voice, presumably imitating Keziah. "'He is just SO handsome. Tall, dark, and handsome. And rich.'"

"Rich. That's interesting. Did she happen to mention what kind of car he drove? A Beemer or something?"

Wilma thought a moment. "Nah. We never saw him or his car. I—well—I thought he'd just sent her pictures online. I've heard about old creepy guys who send pictures of some good-lookin' dude and pretend it's them."

"But now you think they actually met?"

"They must have. Or she wouldn't have left." Wilma took a Kleenex, pushed her glasses up, and blotted her eyes.

"Do you know where they met?"

"Someplace in Alamo, I guess," she mumbled. "We'd have seen them if they'd met in Cloudcroft. Everybody in town would have seen them."

"Do you think Keziah told anyone besides you and your friends about her plans?"

"Huh! I doubt it. I don't think she even told her sister."

"Okay. When she did talk to you all, were you always together?"

Wilma wrinkled her brow. "No. You mean, could she have told us each different things?"

"Not intentionally. But say she had a class with you, for instance, she might have thought of something she wanted to talk about without waiting till everyone else was there."

"Hmm. I suppose so," she said slowly. "But not in class. She wasn't in any of our classes. But after school, when we went to the Teen Center, we didn't always go at the same time. Like, Dot has to baby-sit her little brother on Tuesdays, and Phyllis usually has piano lessons on Thursdays. I guess she got out of them today. I'm usually there unless I have to go to the dentist or something."

"Were the others around when she mentioned Frank's name?"

"Yeah. Well, maybe not Dot. But Phyllis was there."

"Can you think of anything she might have said when the others weren't around? Something that would shed light on this whole situation?"

Wilma's shoulders drooped. "Nah. I didn't always pay that much attention, to tell you the truth."

"Don't worry about it. You've already given us something we didn't know before. Frank's name. And if anything else comes to mind, you can always give me a call."

Wilma smiled, the first time I'd seen her features lighten, the first time I'd thought of her as pretty.

* * *

Tom motioned for me to wait in the office while he took Wilma back into the waiting room. A minute later he came back with Phyllis, and we all seated ourselves.

"Phyllis, if you'd like for your mother to sit in with you, that's okay," Tom said. "Just so you know it's *your* choice."

"No! I'm glad you asked her to wait. It would make me nervous. More nervous. I'm a little nervous already," she said with a slight giggle. "But Dot said it wasn't bad."

Tom grinned. "Good for Dot! Okay, let's get started. I know Joel helped Keziah set up email accounts. Maybe you can fill me in on some of the details. Did Joel know why she wanted them?"

"I think she told him it was just a game. Joel's pretty smart. So I guess he must have figured it out after a while. But I've never talked to him about it."

The basics of Phyllis's version matched Dot and Wilma's, but each girl had relayed the story in her own way, from her own memory, so the answers were nothing like the pat script they'd offered originally.

"Do you know the name of the person she planned to run away with?" Tom asked.

"Franklin. I thought that was his last name, but she said it wasn't. She didn't tell us his last name."

"Do you know where they met?"

Phyllis squirmed in her chair and began jiggling one foot. "Kind of."

I closed my eyes and took a quick breath. *Please, Phyllis, don't back down now.*

"Could I have a drink of water?" she asked.

"Sure," Tom said. "I'll be right back. Sharon, can I get you anything?"

"Mm. Yeah. Dr. Pepper if you have it."

I assumed there was a small kitchen area, or at least a vending machine somewhere in the building. While Tom went in search of our drinks, I spoke to Phyllis.

"Are you still nervous, honey?"

"A little. Kezzie told me some things she didn't tell the others, and I guess I still feel, like, kind of funny talking about them."

"That's natural. Do you think she'd mind if you told them now?"

Phyllis thought that over. "No. Franklin isn't worth keeping a secret about."

She didn't bother trying to hide her tears as the others had done.

CHAPTER 31

Tom returned with our drinks a few minutes later. By then Phyllis was ready to talk again.

"He picked her up at a gas station near Jemma's," she said, as if there hadn't been any interruption in the conversation. "I don't know which one."

"Do you know where they went from there?"

"No. She talked about going to California."

"Where was Jemma?"

"She was waitressing that night."

"Which night was that?"

"Friday the 13th. Or maybe the 14th. It just seemed like a bad-luck day afterwards."

"Okay, let me get this straight. Keziah was supposed to be staying with Jemma?"

Phyllis nodded, and a fresh flow of tears began. I put my hand on her shoulder and handed her a few tissues. Tom and I waited.

"This is the part I don't want my mother to know," she whispered. Then she cleared her throat and spoke in a low voice. "Kezzie left Jemma a note that she was spending the night with me. Of course we knew Jemma would call my mother, so I, like, waited by the phone in my room.

"I picked it up on the first ring. I was afraid Mom would pick up the extension, but when it didn't ring anymore I guess she thought it was a wrong number. Anyway I pretended I was her and said yes, Kezzie was here and did she want to talk to her."

"What would you have done if she'd said yes?" I asked.

"I don't know. Tried to imitate her voice I guess. I'm good at voices. But I was pretty sure she wouldn't take me up on it, 'cause I think she didn't want Kezzie to know she was spying on her. In fact, she said no and please don't say anything to Kezzie about it. I said I sure understand, which is what my mother would have said."

"Didn't the school call the Porters when Keziah didn't show up Monday morning?"

Phyllis licked her lips and began fidgeting again. "I called the school first thing, before they had a chance. I can make my voice, like, real raspy. I told them I was Mrs. Porter and Kezzie had the flu."

I was surprised Phyllis would be this open about their scheming, but Tom kept his poker face intact, and I was practicing mine.

"Do you know if she saw anyone else besides Franklin on the nights she was staying with Jemma?" Tom asked.

"She went out maybe one or two other times. But she was always home by the time Jemma got back."

"So she didn't meet that many guys after all."

"I think she met a lot online, but not in person."

"Did she have anything to say about the ones she met in person?"

"Not a lot. She said they were old. Not like their pictures. And one was real weird."

"Did she elaborate? Say how old they were? Or what seemed weird about one of them?"

"She didn't say how old. But the one that was weird, she made us laugh when she talked about him."

"Go on. The description could help."

Phyllis wrinkled her brow. "She said he looked like Ichabod Crane with a scrawny neck and a big Adam's apple. And he wore glasses and had a mustache that looked fake. I think she said it, like, tilted. And he asked if—" Phyllis blushed— "if her boobs were real. They're kinda big. She left after that."

"Well, I'm glad she did something smart," Tom said casually. "Did these other guys pick her up at the gas station too?"

"Probably."

"Do you know where they went?"

"Some bar near the edge of town. I don't know the name. She said she didn't have to worry about running into anyone she knew."

"Shouldn't be too hard to find. Now tell me more about Franklin."

"I guess they really hit if off. They talked on the phone all the time. But I think they only had, like, one date before they decided to run off and get married."

"And that's when you and your friends got worried?"

"Yeah. Dot told her she was stupid. And Wilma didn't say anything, just gave her one of her looks. Kezzie said didn't I think it was romantic, and I said yes, even though I didn't, because I didn't want to hurt her feelings."

Which explains how you got roped into the plan.

"Maybe you can help me get a timeline on Keziah's comings and goings," Tom said, pulling a legal pad toward him and jotting a few notes. "Up until she met Franklin, did you see her every day?"

"Just about. Except when I had piano lessons. Her mother didn't like her going to the Teen Center, but the school told her she had to. But she only got to stay an hour, and then her mother would pick her up. Or sometimes Jemma would. When it was Jemma's turn, she could stay longer, because Jemma didn't get off work till 5:00."

"When did she meet with Joel?"

"About once or twice a week. Always Fridays and maybe one other day. See, her mother thought she had to go to night classes on Fridays. That's stupid. Teachers can't wait to go home on Fridays. They wouldn't have extra school."

Tom hid a smile. "But her mother believed her?"

"I guess so."

"So Jemma always picked her up on Fridays?"

"Yeah. Kezzie'd leave Joel's before Jemma got off work from the dentist and go back to the Teen Center. But Jemma came early one day and found out about Joel. She was really mad, and they had a big blowup."

Tom quit writing and twirled the pen between his hands. "Did Jemma always work at the restaurant on Fridays?"

"Most of the time."

"Anything else?"

"I don't think so."

Tom stood. "Well, thank you, Phyllis. You've helped a lot. Now we have a little more to go on."

"You won't tell my mother, will you?"

"I don't see any need to."

Tom walked Phyllis to the waiting room, then said he'd take a short break before seeing Joel, who looked noticeably agitated.

I was glad for a chance not only to stretch, but to check in on Ryan, who was engaged in a game of Hangman with Wilma. Dot had gone outside to smoke, and Charlene was pretending to look at a magazine.

Seeing Phyllis's tear-stained face, she rose and gave her a hug. "My goodness, you were in there a long time!"

"Was I?"

"Longer than the others."

"I knew Kezzie better than they did. But it's okay, Mom, so don't worry. We can leave as soon as Joel's had his turn."

CHAPTER 32

I returned to Tom's office to ask if he wanted me in on Joel's session.

"Definitely. But stay in here till I come back—if you don't mind."

"Not at all. That's why I came."

"Let the fun begin," he whispered before leaving the room.

When Joel entered, he looked on the verge of apoplexy, sweat breaking out on his weasely face.

"Have a seat, Joel," Tom said mildly, gesturing to the chair next to mine, before taking his place behind his desk.

"I want my own lawyer!" Joel demanded, still standing.

"Then call him." Tom moved the phone toward Joel.

"He can't just come on the spur of the moment, ya know."

Tom feigned surprise. "You mean you didn't call him before you left home?"

"I take the fifth."

The lawyer in me couldn't resist intervening. "Joel, you can't incriminate yourself unless you've done something incriminating. You haven't, have you?"

He tried glaring at me, but I noticed his lower lip trembling.

"I don't think you have anything to hide," I said, crossing my fingers. "So why don't you see what Sgt. Alderete has to ask before deciding whether or not you need a lawyer. He's not trying to trip you up. He just wants to find out more about Keziah. The focus is on her, not you."

Tom took the cue. "I'm not interested in whether or not you hacked into anyone's computer. Or anything else illegal you might have done. Tell you what." Tom went to the cabinet and pulled out a small camcorder. "Just for you, I'm going to record this meeting."

While Joel fidgeted, Tom set up the camcorder so that we were all in range. He turned it on and began with the usual preliminaries: date, time, names of participants, and our "supposed" willingness to be there.

"Okay, Joel, let's get started. Can you tell me about your relationship with Keziah Porter?"

"What are you implying?" Joel answered sullenly.

"I'm simply asking if you and Keziah were friends, boyfriend and girlfriend, relatives, classmates, or acquaintances. How would you define your relationship?"

"Classmates."

"Good. So you went to school together. And you got together after school to study sometimes?"

Joel thought that over, probably looking for some sinister hidden meaning. Finally, "Yeah. Sometimes."

"Good. Do you know if she had any boyfriends at school?"

"No."

"No, you don't know, or no, she didn't have any."

"You're confusing me."

"Okay, let's move on. Did she ever talk to you about her friends, either at school or outside of school?"

"No."

"Well, that about wraps it up. Thanks for coming in."

Joel looked more puzzled than pleased. "That's all? I can go now?"

"Yep." Tom stood and gave Joel a truly dazzling movie-star smile. I remembered we were on camera and thought to give a fake smile of my own.

As soon as Joel was safely out the door, Tom turned off the camcorder and winked at me. "We can talk later."

Then Tom opened the door and called after Joel, "Oh, by the way, bring your lawyer next time."

* * *

"My, that was quick," Charlene said, as we joined everyone in the waiting room.

Altogether, Tom had probably spent less than 45 minutes interviewing the kids, but the winter sun had already set. Ryan suggested we get something to eat while we were in town, an idea that we all seconded.

Charlene looked at her watch. "It's still a little early. Would it be all right if we made a quick trip to Walmart first?"

Everyone agreed to that plan too, and we set out. Wilma and Dot called home to clear it with their parents, but Joel said his parents were expecting him late anyway. I wondered why. Had he imagined some long drawn-out drama in which he made Sgt. Alderete grovel with apologies? Tom had been wise to use the camcorder, for his own sake, not for Joel's.

* * *

Everyone scattered at Walmart, agreeing to meet at the front entrance by Santa's reindeer in thirty minutes. Ryan headed for the auto-parts section, just to look around. I couldn't think of anything I'd forgotten to bring with me, so browsed the aisles with Charlene instead.

She stopped suddenly in front of the Rice Krispies. "Oh, look over there. It's Mrs. Porter. Poor thing. She must feel awful."

Mrs. Porter appeared to be studying the various types of oatmeal. Next thing I knew, Charlene wheeled her shopping cart toward her. I followed along, both curious and apprehensive.

From what I'd heard, I expected Keziah and Jemma's mother to look like a bona fide witch. Instead, she was rather plain-looking, with pasty skin and hair pulled back in a mousy bun. Her faded brown dress hung loosely on her thin frame.

Charlene touched her on the arm. "I'm so sorry about your daughter. What a terrible loss!"

Mrs. Porter faced Charlene. "I have no daughter. And you have no right to speak to me!" She spoke barely above a whisper, but the venom in her voice and the malice in her eyes were unmistakable.

I felt goosebumps rise on my arms, and Charlene stepped back as though she'd been struck.

Mrs. Porter ranted on about wrath and damnation, ending with, "Save your pity for your own daughter." Spittle had gathered in the corners of her lips. "She's evil, just like the rest of them."

This brought out Charlene's mother-tiger instincts, though she was still shivering. "My daughter doesn't need pity—yours or anyone else's!"

I became aware that Dot had drawn up beside me, her face drained of color. I put my arm around her.

"These girls are not evil, and neither was Keziah," I said evenly.

Just as I'd anticipated, Mrs. Porter turned her malevolence toward me. "Satan has you in his power too!"

"Nope," I said with a cheerfulness I hoped covered my quivering insides. The impact of her poison had stunned me more than I liked to admit. "I didn't give him permission." I turned my back on the vile woman. "Come on, ladies," I said to Charlene and Dot. "Let's go."

CHAPTER 33

We walked away from Mrs. Porter as far and as briskly as our rubbery legs would take us. It occurred to me that I'd been wrong in thinking Alvina had inherited all the leftover mean bones. Compared to Mrs. Porter, Alvina seemed downright saintly.

We reached the toothpaste aisle, which was relatively empty, and stopped to catch our breath.

"Too bad we can't take a shower here," I said in an attempt to lighten the mood—though I knew it would take more than a few jokes to shake off our encounter with Keziah's mother. Dot still looked stunned.

"Let's see. Maybe a Kleenex would work." I took a tissue out of my purse and patted my face and neck.

Charlene, bless her, took up the banter. "I have something even better. I'm buying some of those towelette things you use to wipe off makeup." She reached into her shopping cart, pulled out the box, and opened it. Then she handed us each a small square of damp cloth. She slipped off her coat and used her towelette to wipe her face and arms.

I followed her example.

"Come on, Dot. You too," Charlene said, so Dot shrugged and went along with it.

When we saw how silly we looked, standing in the middle of Walmart scrubbing ourselves with such vigor, we began laughing with the kind of overdone, out-of-place laughter that can border on hysteria.

"I think I'll finish shopping another time," Charlene said between giggles as we started for the register.

Joel scowled at us when we got together again. "What's so funny?"

"We're just trying not to vomit," Dot said, which started us laughing again.

"You were talking about me, weren't you."

"No, Joel, everything isn't about you. We were talking to Kezzie's mother." With that, Dot burst into tears, stalked away from the rest of us and headed for the restroom.

"Do you think we should follow her?" Charlene asked anxiously.

"Let's give her some time alone," I said. "If she's not back in a few minutes, we can check on her."

"I'm going in there with her," Wilma said, walking away from us.

"Me too," Phyllis echoed, joining her.

"I think the three of them will work things out," I told Charlene. "They should be back by the time you've gone through the check-out line."

* * *

Everything seemed to be on an even keel by the time we left for dinner at Margo's. We enjoyed our meal and began the trip home. Charlene and Phyllis decided to run a few more errands, so once again Ryan and I had the same crew we'd started out with.

Joel barged into the back seat first and scrunched against the window. This time Wilma was in the middle, with Dot by the other window, behind Ryan. No one said much at first. Then Dot said, "I hope I don't have nightmares tonight."

"He was rough on you?" Joel asked.

"What are you talking about?"

"The interrogation."

I bit my tongue.

"Oh, yeah," Dot said sarcastically. "Bamboo sticks in my fingernails. No, stupid. I mean about The Witch."

"What about her?"

"We ran into her at Walmart. I didn't hear what Ms. Wood said, but it sure set her off."

"Ms. Wood did what any normal person would do," I said. "She offered Mrs. Porter sympathy."

"After the way Mrs. Porter treated her last time, I was surprised Ms. Wood even spoke to her," Dot said.

I turned partway in my seat so I could smile at her. "Ms. Wood is simply a kind person."

"Yeah. She's cool. Even if she's kinda nosy sometimes."

"Dot, remember when you told me about that first time they had a run-in?" I asked. "Did it bother you as much then as it did this time?"

Dot shuddered. "It was kinda creepy, but I didn't look at her face last time. So I just thought she was, like, nuts. But this time...her face...I can't get it out of my mind. And I sure don't want to dream about it."

"I only saw her once," Joel said. "Kezzie always waited for her about half a block away from the Teen Center. That day Mrs. Porter was early, and we almost didn't get back in time. She started screaming, calling Kezzie names, I guess 'cause she was with me."

For a few moments, I sympathized with Joel, and my opinion of him softened.

"Poor Kezzie," Dot said. "The Witch didn't want her to have any friends. She didn't even like her to hang out with her sister."

"That's because Jemma's a lesbian," Joel said in his know-it-all way. "Mrs. Porter thought Jemma'd turn Kezzie into a lesbian too."

"She'd have better luck turning her into a pumpkin," I said tartly.

Dot snorted. "Joel, you are so stupid."

"It could happen," he insisted.

"She could turn into a pumpkin?"

"No, smartass. You know what I mean."

"Just shut up, both of you," Wilma said, and they all lapsed into silence for the rest of the ride back to Cloudcroft.

CHAPTER 34

After dropping off the kids at their respective homes, Ryan and I stopped in the lounge to unwind with a glass of Chardonnay.

"What a day!" I said, stretching briefly before we sank into the comfortable chairs.

"What happened with Mrs. Porter?" Ryan asked, after we'd spent a few minutes quietly savoring our wine. "Or would you rather not talk about it."

"Maybe talking will help cut it down to size." I told Ryan about the encounter, which did lose some of its power in the telling. "I guess it's one of those 'you-had-to-be-there' things. Like Dot said, it was seeing the hate in her face that chilled us so." I shivered involuntarily. "Not that her words weren't horrible enough."

"No wonder Dot worried about nightmares. Tell me about Tom's talks with the kids, or are they confidential?"

"Not really. Well, maybe a few things are," I added, thinking of Phyllis's schemes to cover for Keziah. "But mostly the girls were pretty open." I related the gist of the interviews and my appreciation of Tom's low-key approach. "I didn't really have anything to offer—except moral support. Didn't find it necessary to mention that I don't practice law in New Mexico."

Ryan laughed. "Sneaky."

I laughed with him. "I suppose it would have been, if I'd done any practicing, if maybe I'd jumped in and shouted, 'I object' now and then. Oh, I also forgot to mention that I don't practice criminal law either. That would have been for Joel's benefit."

"What about him?"

"Waste of time. What little time he wasted. One thing that struck me. All the girls seem genuinely distressed about Keziah's death, and all feel some degree of remorse for not doing more for her. But Joel hasn't shown any regrets over anything—none that I can see anyway. It's just so odd, even if they were 'only classmates,' which is what he claimed."

"Well, you're not the only armchair psychologist. I think Tom and I both qualify. I wondered if Tom made Joel wait till last on purpose. He got more and more wound up the later it got. I'd hate to go so far as to call him a sociopath. Could be he's 'merely' narcissistic."

"Hmm. That's something to think about.... Okay, your turn. Tell me how everything went in the waiting room."

"It went. None of them said anything about the interviews—maybe because Charlene Wood and I were there. But Dot was in a great mood when she came out. She talked my ear off, mostly about school stuff." Ryan gave me a wicked grin. "She thinks I'm probably a great teacher and wishes I'd teach in Cloudcroft."

"You *are* a great teacher, and you've undoubtedly bewitched her. I've never seen her so vivacious."

"She's cute. She'll be a knockout when she grows up and fixes her hair."

"Now that she's met you, she might even fix it sooner," I teased. "What about the other kids?"

"Wilma seemed a little withdrawn before her session. Still quiet afterwards, but noticeably relieved. She can be very direct, but funny. I didn't know how she'd take to playing something as simple as Hangman, but we both enjoyed it."

"Phyllis?"

"She didn't have much to say. Charlene's nice, but I think she hovers too much."

"Back to Joel. What was going on with him?"

"Not much to add. He didn't say anything to anyone before his interview, just got more and more jumpy. Afterwards he looked a little dazed, but we cleared the waiting room shortly after that. So his reaction got lost in the shuffle."

"Not that I put much stock in anything he says, but I wonder if it's true that Jemma's a lesbian. It would explain why the girls were so secretive the other day when someone said Mrs. Porter thought Keziah would end up like her sister. Brenda said it was because Mrs. P. was afraid Keziah would learn to think for herself. But somehow I felt there was more to it."

"I'll tell you what I wonder about Jemma," Ryan said. "I don't see how she could live in that household and come out unscarred. Instead, she's an honor student, self-reliant, conscientious. Almost too good to be true."

"I don't know. She is a little bitter around the edges, On the other hand, it sounds like she has a lot of really good friends. Tom, Cindy—their whole family. The Taylors, the people who helped her break away. Good odds for survival, I'd say."

* * *

The symposium kept me busy till mid-afternoon Friday. Meanwhile, Ryan welcomed a little down-time to settle in with a book on El Paso history.

At noon, I returned a call Tom had left earlier. We exchanged "call-me" messages for a while till he finally reached me shortly after the legal sessions had ended for the day.

"You probably noticed," he began, "that one of Keziah's 'dates' kind of matched the description Ms. Piffle had given us about the guy she chased into El Paso."

"I did, but I put it out of my mind. Alvina's interpretation of things isn't always too reliable."

"That was my impression at first. But then I thought maybe it was too coincidental to ignore. Will and I discussed it, and we'd like to talk to her again."

"I'm sure she'd welcome being in the limelight again!"

"Her cousin was very protective, but we did set up a meeting for this afternoon. I wondered if you'd like to be in on it."

"Sure. If it's okay with her."

"We'll see how it goes. We'll be up there about 4:00. Does that work for you?"

"You bet."

We ended our call, and I told Ryan about the unexpected outcome of yesterday's interview with Phyllis.

CHAPTER 35

I met with Mela and Alvina in the lobby about an hour before Tom was due. Mela wore an electric-blue pantsuit with matching pointy shoes and a bright purple and blue bandeau. A feather sprouted from the bandeau, making me think of the roaring twenties. Alvina wore yet another dowdy sweatsuit with matching oxfords. I wondered how many gray outfits she owned. At least she was beginning to heal, her bruises beginning to fade.

I hadn't talked with them since day before yesterday and was curious to know if their trip to El Paso had been productive.

Mela said yes and Alvina said no simultaneously.

"Allie's car isn't beyond repair, but the estimates we got were unbelievably expensive—more than the insurance could cover. We stopped at a dealership I trust and found some nice cars at a comparable price. But Allie was getting tired, so we left without deciding anything."

"I was not getting tired. Maybe *you* left without deciding anything. If the prices are so damn comparable, it makes sense to get my old car back. And that's what *I* decided to do."

"Well, you don't have to make your mind up right away."

"Did you do anything else while you were in town?" I said, thinking a change of subject might ward off a no-win argument.

Again, Mela said yes and Alvina said no simultaneously.

"We stopped at my boutique," Mela said. "Oh, did Caterina happen to tell you? I'm part-owner of a small boutique in Cielo Vista Mall. Silent partner, really."

"Melina's husband is rich, so she doesn't have to work," Alvina muttered.

Mela ignored her. "I'd thought a new wardrobe might cheer Allie up. Or if not a whole wardrobe, at least a couple of new dresses."

"I'd look like an idiot in those things you picked out."

"Did you have lunch at Cappetto's?" I asked, searching for a safe, pleasant subject. "I don't think we thanked you for recommending it, Mela. Our meals were delicious!"

"I'm allergic to Italian food," Alvina said.

Mela rolled her eyes. This week had seemed short to me, but I suspect it was beginning to seem rather long to Mela with her self-imposed chore of caring for her cousin.

"We ate at Luby's," Mela said. "They have an excellent buffet—plenty of dishes to choose from."

Plenty of dishes for Alvina to find fault with.

"I suppose Sgt. Alderete told you he'd asked me to join you when he comes here this afternoon," I said.

"Don't know why," Alvina grumbled. "Does he think I need a lawyer?"

"Heavens, no. I imagine since you and I both saw the man you followed—" *or think you followed—* "Sgt. Alderete might assume I have something helpful to offer."

"That's a wonderful idea!" Mela gushed. "He sounds like a very conscientious young man. Or is he an old man? Mercy me, everyone is so young nowadays—doctors, policemen, lawyers. Even Father Nicolas can't be a day over thirty."

"Nobody wants to hear about your church, Melina. I hope you won't take up the sergeant's time yakking about trivia. As for you—" Alvina gave me an icy stare— "don't interrupt when you don't even know what you're talking about."

I winked at Mela. "Shall we behave?"

Mela threw back her head, causing the feather to wobble a bit, and laughed, a loud infectious sound of glee. "Oh my, yes. I wouldn't dream of interfering!"

* * *

Sheriff Gibson and Tom arrived shortly before 4:00 and arranged with the staff to use a private room downstairs for the interview.

"Your information might be quite helpful, Ms. Piffle," Sheriff Gibson began after we'd gathered together and were all seated around a small rectangular table.

"I told you that to begin with," she snapped.

"So you did." Sheriff Gibson opened a manila folder and took out a copy of the report she'd made Tuesday. "We hope you might recall details that hadn't occurred to you earlier. Would you mind telling us—again—your first impression of the man you followed to El Paso?"

"He was guilty. You could see it in his face."

"Guilty of...?"

"Being a pervert." Impatience rang in her voice.

"I see." Sheriff Gibson looked down at the report and scribbled a note in the margin. "How else would you describe him? Hair color, eye color—?"

"I already told you."

"Brown hair, thinning," the sheriff read from the report. "Brown eyes, glasses." He turned to me. "Anything to add?"

Oh, that's right. My input is supposed to be significant too.

"I just caught a glimpse of him, but I do remember his glasses. Square with black rims. They seemed a little large for his face. Not that I gave it much thought at the time...."

Sheriff Gibson nodded. "Sometimes things are clearer in retrospect." He turned back to Alvina. "Did you have that same impression? About the glasses being too large?"

"Hmph. What I remember is that the lenses looked clear—too clear. Like he didn't really need them. That's why I recognized him without them."

"Good. This is starting to add up. What about height? Was he as tall as, say, Sgt. Alderete?"

"No. Taller. I came up to his shoulder, and I'm five-two."

Sheriff Gibson raised his eyebrows. I wondered if we were both surprised that she'd answered two questions in a row without being abrasive. He made a notation on the back of the report. "Good. That narrows it down even further. Did you notice anything else? Scars, tattoos, cuts, bruises?"

A prominent Adam's apple?

"Nope. Wouldn't have seen 'em even if he'd had 'em. He wore a long-sleeved turtleneck." She paused. "I did see a tiny cut on his jaw."

"Like he'd nicked it shaving?"

Alvina's eyes flashed. "That's why I knew his mustache was fake when I saw him later. He didn't have one at Ernie's."

The sheriff tapped his pencil against the side of the table while he seemed to sort out what he'd heard. "Okay, he was wearing a turtleneck at Ernie's. How about when you saw him later?"

"He had on a heavy coat and a hood. But that didn't keep me from recognizing him!" she added defiantly.

"No. You're very observant," he assured her. Then he addressed Tom: "Do you think we can get Desi to work up a sketch for us?"

"I don't see why not. Maybe more than one picture: One with mustache, one without. Dressed different ways."

"Did you talk to him either time you saw him?" Sheriff Gibson asked Alvina.

"At Ernie's."

"And?"

She pulled herself up to her full five-two. "I asked him how long he thought he could go on hiding. He wouldn't answer. Played dumb. Pulled some money out of his wallet and put it on the table, then left."

So. He paid for lunch after all. Maybe even alleged perverts have a conscience of sorts.

CHAPTER 36

Sheriff Gibson opened his briefcase and pulled out another folder. He opened it to display six wallet-sized photographs, which he slid toward Alvina and me. "I wanted to hear your own observations before showing you these. But—to save time and another trip—we came up with some pictures that matched your earlier description of the man in question. Can you tell us if there's anyone here you recognize?"

"All a bunch of perverts," Alvina grumbled. "Just round up the whole bunch."

"I wish we could do that," the sheriff agreed amiably, "but for now we'll have to focus on just one of them."

I saw Bulldog's face right away, but knew that I recognized him from the picture I'd seen online earlier and not necessarily because he looked like the man we'd seen at Ernie's. The other faces had various points of similarity either to him or to the "weird" date Keziah had made fun of to her friends.

The differences kept me from making a positive match. The guy with the scrawny neck also had large ears. Another man wore rimless glasses that revealed pale blue eyes. Not that he couldn't have changed the color with contacts. The one who looked most like Mr. Nondescript had a receding hairline. Then again, I suppose he could have worn a toupee along with his supposed fake mustache. Another easy change.

I waited for Alvina to speak first, half-expecting her to make one of her typical snap judgments, but after eliminating three of the pictures from the start, she examined the others carefully. In the end, she identified Bulldog, but only tentatively. Maybe she was taking this assignment seriously. Maybe because she herself was being taken seriously for once.

"We might not need a sketch after all," Tom said. "We can alter the photo itself—add glasses, a mustache, etc. Then show you the new pictures."

"You mean, make another trip?" Alvina asked.

"It should go quickly next time," Tom assured her. "Either it'll help, or it won't. And we'll have a better idea where to go from there."

And where would that be, I wondered. Even if we made a positive ID of the man Alvina followed, it didn't mean he'd turned on her and caused her accident. And where was the connection to Keziah, if any?

Mela had been listening attentively to the conversation. She'd looked over Alvina's shoulder during the photo-viewing, but—true to her word—had "behaved herself" and kept quiet up till now.

"I'd like to be able to recognize this man too," she said, tapping the page of photos with a sharp red fingernail, "in case we run into him again. We're planning to leave for El Paso tomorrow. We'll stop at your office on the way to take a look at your souped-up photos."

"Good." Sheriff Gibson collected the photos and the report, stuffed them back into his briefcase and rose to go. "What time?"

After some discussion, during which it was obvious Mela and Alvina weren't in agreement about when they'd leave, Mela promised to call the sheriff "first thing tomorrow morning."

* * *

Sheriff Gibson motioned for me to stay after Alvina and Mela left the room. "I should probably deputize you," he said with a chuckle. "That would put us all on a first-name basis. I'm Will, by the way."

"I'm glad to skip the formality too. I'm Sharon."

"Tom has told me how helpful you've been. And discreet. We felt like we'd been wading through quicksand ever since Keziah disappeared. Thanks to you, those girls finally came forward and gave us something to work with."

"I think they'd have talked to you sooner or later anyway."

"Well, you made it sooner, so maybe we'll get unstuck. Unfortunately, new problems seem to crop up faster than old ones get resolved." Will took off his glasses, polished them with his handkerchief, then held them up to the light, apparently examining them for wayward specks, before putting them on again. Laugh lines around his brown eyes belied the sadness I saw in them now.

Will cleared his throat, then leaned forward, his hands folded on the table. "The autopsy report came in. It's public record, of course, but we're not volunteering anything. Not until we have to."

Tom stared straight ahead, as if he could recite facts without thinking about them. "The official ruling was 'asphyxia'—most likely, she was smothered to death. Among other things, there were signs of hemorrhaging in the eyes."

I flinched at Tom's bluntness, though I knew it couldn't have been any easier for him.

"Sorry to be so clinical," he said. "I'll stop if you want me to."

"No, that's okay. I really do want to know what happened."

"Well, unofficially, the attacker must have been very strong to keep Keziah from fighting back. Or she could have been drugged. Tox results aren't in yet."

"Do they know how long she'd been dead? Or where she was killed?"

"Time of death was hard to pin down, thanks to the weather. Judging from the contents of her stomach, they figured she hadn't been dead more than a day or so. And judging by the position of the body and other factors, they think she was killed somewhere else and dumped out on that mountain."

Vivid pictures flitted through my imagination, causing my stomach to knot up. "If there were any signs she'd been dragged through the snow," I said, trying to match Tom's detached approach, "we skied over them." My face reddened at the memory of our carelessness.

"You can quit blaming yourselves for that," Will put in. "More than likely, they used the same service road we did. Snowmobilers use that road all the time, so it would be hard to isolate fresh tracks. Anyway, we're just glad you found her when you did." He paused. "There's another odd thing, if you want to call it that. She'd apparently been undressed, then dressed again. Carelessly, as if the perp was in a hurry. Underpants on crooked, but no sign of sexual activity...unless you want to count...there were signs her wrists had been bound. Rope burns."

Kinky. I tried to push the pictures away from my mind and keep the room from spinning. "That *is*...strange," I said with a calmness I didn't feel. "Easy to speculate though. Maybe she wouldn't. Maybe her attacker couldn't."

"Like you say, lots of room for speculation," Tom said. "Could be she and Joel were fooling around. Doesn't mean he killed her. Then there's Bulldog—very likely impotent. But violence doesn't fit the profile."

"You never know what tips the scales," Will said. "We only heard one side of the story about Miss Keziah finding him weird. Nothing says rejection like walking out on someone. Who knows? On top of that, she might have made some flip remark he stewed over."

"So is that why you're looking to see if Alvina's description of the man she tracked down matches Keziah's?"

"Yes. Not to minimize Ms. Piffle's accident, but—solving that is kind of a lost cause."

"Kind of like finding the elusive Franklin." Tom said. "Backing up, remember when Phyllis said Keziah talked to him on the phone 'all the time'?"

"I remember."

"Well, we found Keziah's cell phone under her body—smashed to pieces. Smashed with a hammer, it looked like. No fingerprints on what was left of it."

I shivered. "I can understand why someone might destroy it. But why not just throw it away afterwards? And if her body was moved to the mountain after she'd been killed, why bring the phone along?"

"We were counting on your armchair psychology to figure it out," Tom said, half-kiddingly.

"Hmm. More speculation. The killer's way of letting you know you can never trace the calls? Can never find him? Or maybe some anger directed toward Keziah in a warped kind of way. What do you think?"

"Pretty much the same. We lean toward the first theory—that it's his way of showing he has the upper hand.

But it could have something to do with Keziah too. A symbol of some kind."

"Regret?"

"Possibly. Most likely, it's something more self-serving."

A sudden deep chill invaded my whole being, while a disconnected phrase filled my mind: *It's significant.*

CHAPTER 37

What is significant? I wondered. The phone?

"Is it cold in here?" I asked Will and Tom, even as the chill dissipated.

Tom gave me a quizzical look. "No. In fact, I was thinking it seemed a little warm."

Will nodded agreement.

I'd never thought of myself as psychic, but this was the second supposed "message" that had come out of nowhere, accompanied by an unexplained wave of frigid air.

"Are you okay?" Tom asked. "You look a little pale."

Unsettled is more like it. "I'm just...trying to process things. Um, have you ever thought of consulting a psychic?"

Will's eyes glazed over; no "woo-woo" stuff for him. But Tom's gaze intensified. I didn't know how to interpret it. Strong feelings, perhaps, but for or against the idea?

Will looked at his watch. "We should get going. My wife'll be expecting me for dinner, and Tom has a heavy date later on."

The mundane words brought me back to myself. "You mean you have lives outside of law enforcement?" I said lightly.

Tom grinned. "Only on Friday nights...and Sundays, and maybe Saturdays, Tuesdays, or Thursdays."

Will laughed. "We wind up doing a lot of flex time."

"But never on Sunday afternoons," Tom said. "Dinner here in town with my mom and dad and all the crew. That's strictly non-flex."

"Sunday. Day after tomorrow," I mused. "Just a few more days and we'll be going back home. I hope you'll keep me posted about...." I groped for words. Somehow saying "Keziah's case" sounded too detached. And I'd gotten much too involved. "How everything turns out," I added lamely.

"Hey, you're part of our team," Tom said. "And we still haven't finished picking your brain."

"Lotsa luck. I think my brain is operating on overdrive."

And that would explain those telepathic flashes—if that's what they were. Brain deprived of oxygen too early in the morning, and again too late in the afternoon. As good an explanation as any.

"You say you'll be here a few more days?" Tom asked.

"Yes. The symposium officially ends after breakfast tomorrow. Then Ryan and I are going up to Ski Apache for the rest of the day. We haven't planned much beyond that."

"Oh, you're downhill skiers too?"

"We took lessons in Red River a few years ago. I kept upright long enough to have fun, but I'll probably be a 'green dot' forever. Ryan might brave the more challenging runs."

"It'll be a good change of pace. Now that you mention it, maybe I'll see you up there."

"If you and your husband get around to the black-diamond runs," Will said with a wink.

"Right." I said. "See you there!"

* * *

Saturday morning the sky was blue as only New Mexico skies can be. Royal blue. Cloudless. Enough snow had fallen in the last few days to make the ski runs powdery and inviting.

We rented equipment at the ski area and went outside into the snow. There we donned boots, attached them to skis, and headed for the bunny lift.

"I'll work up to the 'derring-do' stuff after a while," Ryan said. "Right now it's nice just to ski together."

"Yes, it is. And it feels good to exercise. I haven't done much of that lately, unless you want to count walking through Walmart and hospital corridors."

After a few runs on the easy trails, I convinced Ryan that he should ski the intermediate slopes. It didn't take much persuasion. Our "togetherness" consisted of riding the lifts side by side. When it came to actual skiing, he always reached the bottom of the hill before I could get out of my snowplow.

We met up again for lunch at the cafeteria. We'd just gotten through the line when we spotted Tom sitting with a crowd of people at a long table nearby. When he saw us, he waved us over.

After reaching their table with our trays, we sat across from Tom's sister Cindy and her boyfriend, who welcomed us right away. Cindy had short curly hair, light brown like Tom's, and big brown eyes enhanced by long thick lashes.

Tom sat next to Cindy, with an unsmiling brunette named Rowena on his other side. I wondered if she was his "heavy date" from last night, and if she was tired from last night and/or from skiing, or if she was simply bored.

Two of Tom and Cindy's brothers and a few other friends completed the group, and I mentally reviewed names, hoping I could remember them all.

Out of the corner of my eye, I saw someone else waving, and looked across the room to see Dot, a big grin on the visible half of her face. I poked Ryan in the ribs, and we both waved back. Tom turned to follow our exchange, gave a wave of his own, and began chuckling.

Rowena's eyes narrowed to slits as she zeroed in on Dot. "Is that the brat who was trying to out-ski you up on 'Screaming Eagle'?"

"Yeah, big brother," Cindy put in, mischief dancing in her eyes. "She did it too!"

Tom laughed. "She is a daredevil. Guess I'm getting cautious in my old age."

Everyone but Rowena laughed with him.

"Over the hill at twenty-six," Cindy teased. "Hey, I just had an idea. Maybe you and Dot could have a re-match this afternoon."

I think Cindy and I both had an idea how this would go over with Rowena, and I admired how subtly she inserted the needle.

One of Tom's brothers offered to challenge him instead, and the conversation took a boisterous turn, ending with family members goading each other into impossible feats. Rowena's contribution was to roll her eyes at intervals.

After lunch, we started off in different directions. Some of the group had bought half-day tickets and were on their way home. The rest of us were ready to hit the slopes again.

Tom kidded us that we might like to ski the treacherous runs. "There's one I call the White-Knuckle Trail. Sure you don't want to give it a try?"

"You must have seen my moments of glory on the bunny slope," I said.

He laughed. "I did see Ryan, and he's good."

"Yeah," Ryan said. "I don't fall down as much as I used to. How about recommending some trails for fair-to-middlin' skiers?"

While they were discussing this, Cindy stopped me to say she was glad we'd joined them for green-chili burgers. "I've heard such nice things about you from Tom," she said. "And now I know why."

"Thanks. I think a lot of him too."

Dot crossed the room to join us. I would say she swaggered, but it's hard to swagger, or do anything gracefully, in ski boots. "Hey, Cindy, Ms. S."

Cindy smiled at her. "Hey, girl. You really pounded those slopes today."

Dot's face clouded. "Yeah. I forget everything when I'm skiing."

Cindy draped an arm around Dot's shoulder. "I'm sorry about Kezzie."

"We were thinking of going to see Jemma—me and Phyllis." Dot brightened. "You remember, Ms. S.? How Ms. T. thought it would be a good idea to see if Jemma has some of Kezzie's paintings?"

"I do remember. I'm glad you're following up."

"Have you seen Jemma since you got back?" Dot asked Cindy.

"Not too often. She needed some time alone."

"Oh." Dot's face fell. "Maybe we shouldn't go over there yet."

"No, I think you should. I think it would be a good idea. It would be good for her to know Kezzie's friends miss her too. Jemma's still up and down. Either hurting or pretending she's not. So if you catch her at a bad time, just let it go and plan to come back later."

"Would you like to go with us?" Dot asked hopefully.

"We'll see. Give me a call when you're ready to go, and we'll see."

"Okay. My brother's waiting for me. See ya." Dot clunked off in the opposite direction toward a dark-haired boy who looked to be a couple of years older. Nice-looking kid. Made me wonder about Dot's natural hair color.

Cindy cupped her hands over her mouth and yelled after Dot, "Give my brother hell!"

Without turning around, Dot gave an airy wave of acknowledgment.

CHAPTER 38

"Do you have a minute?" Cindy asked me.

"Sure. Those five-year-olds will have to zip up and down the beginner trails without me."

"Oh, don't shortchange yourself. You'll be ready for black diamonds before you know it."

"By the end of the day at least."

"How 'bout let's grab some hot apple cider and go find a place to sit in the lounge. I told Roque I'd catch up with him later."

Ryan and I had already agreed to meet there when we'd finished our respective runs, so I figured he wouldn't miss me. Right now, he and Tom were still discussing the relative merits of black versus blue trails (green not worth mentioning).

After Cindy and I had our cider in hand and had relaxed in cushioned armchairs by the fireplace, we were quiet for a few minutes. I admired the decorations, shimmery garlands strung across the ceiling in graceful curves with shiny red, silver, and gold pear-shaped ornaments hanging from them. I waited for Cindy to tell me what was on her mind.

"It's about Jemma," she said at last. "Tom is a very loyal person, and he expects friendships to go on forever."

"Sometimes friendships—take a detour."

"That's one way of putting it. Jemma and I were good friends all through high school. But then she changed—something changed."

"In what way?"

"I know this sounds weird, but she started to get more like her mother. In the way she treated Kezzie. Like she wanted to control her. Not in a bad way," Cindy hastened to add. "Her intentions were really good. Poor Jemma. She wanted so much to be 'normal.'"

Cindy closed her eyes for a few moments. "Anyway, she wanted Kezzie to be 'normal' too. To have sleepovers with her friends and bake brownies and braid their hair—things she thought 'normal' girls did."

Tears slid down Cindy's face. "The whole thing is so damn sad."

I didn't know how to respond so simply reached over and touched Cindy's hand. She linked her fingers through mine as if she needed something to hold on to.

"Jemma used to spend a lot of time at our house," Cindy said at last. "But she was never allowed to stay all night. So when she moved to Alamo, she finagled it so Kezzie could stay with her once in a while. Then she set up this sleepover soon after school let out for the summer.

"Not many girls came. Charlene Wood drove a few of the girls down to Alamo, mostly so she could check on Jemma's digs and make sure there wouldn't be any alcohol."

Cindy smiled. "It irritated Jemma. But Charlene could report back to the other moms that all was secure. I drove a few girls down, and that was it."

"I get the feeling it didn't work out the way Jemma planned."

"'Jemma planned.' That was the problem. The girls wanted to talk about boys and whoever they were mad at that week. And paint each other's nails and make popcorn and watch videos. Jemma wanted them to listen up while she organized games—charades and some other things. Not that they minded the games. They just didn't want to be organized."

"Was Keziah ever invited to the other girls' sleepovers?"

"Mm. A couple of times that I know of. But Jemma had her nose out of joint over how 'unappreciative' the girls had been at her house. So she wouldn't allow it. And that's probably what started the wall between Jemma and me. I thought she was being unreasonable, and I told her so."

"Sounds like Jemma's a perfectionist."

"She was. But she's also intelligent. It took awhile, but when she realized she'd been too hard on Kezzie, she quit being so hard on herself. That's when she allowed herself to...see Elise."

"Is Elise her partner?"

Cindy stiffened, then studied my face, as if looking to see whether I approved or disapproved of Jemma and Elise's relationship. "I don't know," she said. "I don't know how serious it is. And they still keep it kinda quiet."

"It's hard to keep quiet in a small town. It's hard, period."

The tension eased in Cindy's shoulders. "Tom thinks that's what put a strain on my friendship with Jemma. It bothers him because he's always been like the big brother she never had, so he thinks I should still be like a sister. But it's her call, and she's shut me out."

"I wonder if she'd really welcome Keziah's friends," I said.

"I have no idea. That's one reason I've been telling you all this. I wonder if you'd mind going with the girls if they ask. You could be kind of a buffer."

"Hmm. If Phyllis is going, Charlene is probably driving them down there."

"That would really set Jemma off."

"On second thought, I doubt if Charlene knows they're going. Maybe the girls are planning for Dot's brother to drive them."

"Well, I guess I shouldn't try to control things either. What'll be will be."

CHAPTER 39

Sunday was a good day to unwind. Ryan and I had both planned to spend some leisure time reading, and our vacation was fast slipping away. Besides that, much as we'd enjoyed our ski trip yesterday, we were a tad achy from the unaccustomed maneuvers. Another reason to curl up with good books while Tiger Balm did its magic.

It began snowing about noon—big fat fluffy flakes—and by mid-afternoon we decided to go outside and help some of the other guests build a snowfamily. I was in the middle of making whiskers from pine needles for my snowkitten when my cell phone rang.

It was Dot, asking if she and Phyllis could come over. Dot sounded somewhat subdued—totally unlike herself—and I wondered what was troubling her.

"Sure, come on up."

Next thing I knew, Dot and Phyllis topped the long uphill drive to The Lodge. After taking off their cross-country skis, they joined the rest of us in our snowsculpting endeavors. With their help, my snowkitten, whiskers slightly askew, was finished.

Brushing snow off my gloves, I suggested we go inside for something to warm us up. The girls liked the sound of hot cocoa, so we ordered mugs in the lounge, then sat at a small table to enjoy the sweet foamy beverages.

Not one for small talk, Dot said, "We went to see Jemma. About some of Kezzie's pictures."

"Goodness. You didn't ski all the way down to Alamogordo and back, did you?" I asked.

"No," Phyllis said. "My aunt lives there. So we were already there."

"Visiting your aunt?"

"Yes. We always have dinner at my aunt's after church every Sunday, me and my family. So I called Dot to see if she could, like, get her brother to bring her down if Mom would let us go to Jemma's."

"I take it everything worked out."

"Not exactly. I mean, at first it did. Dot and her brother came down a little after dinner. I told Mom we'd only be gone about thirty or forty minutes, so she said okay." Tears pricked Phyllis's eyelids.

Dot's eyes clouded over too. "We weren't even gone that long. Jemma's a little bossy, but she's always been nice before. Today she was just plain weird."

"When we asked her if we could have some of Kezzie's drawings," Phyllis continued, "her face got all red and blotchy and she kind of yelled that she didn't keep any of Kezzie's stuff, that she'd thrown it all away. So we just got out of there as fast as we could."

I wrapped my hands around my mug, as if I could extract some extra warmth from it. "That *is* strange."

"When my cousin was killed in a hunting accident," Phyllis said, "my aunt left his room exactly the way it was. It's been ten years."

"Yeah, well, I don't think that's healthy either," Dot said.

"Different people handle things different ways," I said, stating the obvious. *And Keziah's family is certainly different.*

"I just don't understand why Jemma'd be in such a hurry to get rid of everything," Phyllis said. "I can see why she might not want to go through it right away, but just to throw it out...."

"Kezzie had some really beautiful pictures too," Dot added.

"Well, I'm as puzzled as you are. But—I wonder—did Keziah take art classes in school? Maybe her teacher kept some of her work."

"I hadn't thought of that!" Phyllis said, relief in her face. "Ms. Lathrop kept all her kids' projects in folios. Then at the end of the year she'd give them back."

"Great! I'm curious, did Keziah do mostly watercolors, oils, charcoal drawings, pen-and-ink drawings—what else?"

"Ms. Lathrop had them doing some of everything," Dot said. "I liked her watercolors best."

"We'll talk with Ms. Lathrop as soon as break's over," Phyllis said. "See if she'll give us something of Kezzie's."

"Sounds like a plan. By the way, where's Wilma?" I asked.

"They left for El Paso as soon as school let out. Just for the weekend. They're supposed to be back tomorrow."

"Well, for now—if you've finished your cocoa—let's go back outside and see who's been added to the snowfamily."

We bundled up again and joined the snowsculptors, hardy souls undaunted by the weather, which had gotten increasingly colder. The snow entourage now included several people, plus a moose and a bear. Dot scooped up some snow to form a snowball, which she threw at Ryan.

"Hey!" he called. "No fair. I'm still working on my masterpiece."

Despite his words, he seemed ready to take a break from his "masterpiece" (which looked something like a deformed coyote). He promptly volleyed a snowball back to Dot, and they laughed, ducked, and/or got splatted by each other for a few minutes. Phyllis and I played cheerleader, rooting for them both.

"I give up!" Ryan said at last. "I'm waving a white flag."

"Your white flag looks like another snowball to me," Dot said.

He grinned. "Guilty!"

"Uh oh," Phyllis said. "Cell-phone alert." She clicked her phone open and looked at the caller ID. "Mom."

After Phyllis answered the call, both girls attached their skis, waved goodbye, and started down the hill again.

"I'll give you another chance tomorrow, Mr. S.," Dot called over her shoulder. "See ya."

CHAPTER 40

Over dinner I told Ryan about the girls' abortive visit to Jemma's. "They were pretty shaken over the incident, so I'm glad they were able to get their minds on something fun before the afternoon ended."

"Yeah. At the expense of my getting clobbered," he teased.

"You held your own. Oh, and I'm sorry you had to give up on your coyote."

"It was a husky," he said in a fake-injured tone.

"I knew that all along."

"Getting back to Jemma," Ryan said, "I'm not surprised she's acting so strange. I think anybody that tightly wound is bound to come unhinged."

"I'm going to call Tom tomorrow. He seems to be the one person she can relate to. Besides Elise, whoever she is."

* * *

Monday morning I phoned Tom bright and early. "Am I still on the team?" I asked, half-jokingly.

"Sure. What's up?"

"It's about Jemma. Her behavior has gotten a little—disturbing."

I heard a sharp intake of breath over the airwaves.

"Would you mind coming by this afternoon?" he asked. "Say, about 1:00? We can talk about it then."

"I'd be glad to. Ryan too?"

"Of course."

* * *

When we arrived, we waited in the reception room while Tom interviewed a woman who claimed to have been abducted by aliens during routine testing at White Sands Missile Range. The door to Tom's office was partly open, since the woman claimed to be claustrophobic as well, so the conversation was hardly secret. We also learned that she suspected a cover-up by the U.S. government and wanted the local authorities to look into the kidnapping instead.

Tom assured her that he and the whole department were working on it, and she left with a smile.

"Her weekly visit," Tom said as he led us into his office. "It doesn't bother her that we never find anything. She's happy as long as she thinks we're trying."

"Good reminder for us that you have other cases besides Keziah's," I said.

"Hers is never far from my mind. Y'know, we try to be objective, but we tough guys take things more to heart than people realize." He motioned for us to sit down, then pulled his chair from behind the desk and sat across from us. "Now, what's this about Jemma?"

"Well, short story short: Dot and Phyllis went to her house to ask for drawings or paintings Keziah had done. Jemma got agitated and told them she hadn't kept *anything* of her sister's."

"Hmm. You think they were telling the truth?"

"I don't know why they'd lie."

"Well, somebody's lying. Yesterday afternoon, Jemma left a message to call her when I came to work this morning. Which I did. She said she hadn't wanted to bother us on the weekend, but someone broke into her house

Saturday night and stole all Keziah's stuff. I don't know why *she*'d lie."

"To you or to the girls?"

Tom's jaw tightened. "To either of us."

I was beginning to think Cindy was right. Tom's loyalty was his blind spot. As if reading my mind, he said, "Will sent someone else to Jemma's to follow up."

"I see. What did he find out?"

Tom shrugged and looked away. "Nothing. Keziah's room was cleaned out. Nothing personal left."

"Was the room left in a mess? As if the thief was careless or in a hurry or something?"

Tom shrugged again. "Didn't seem that way."

"Was anything else stolen?"

Tom looked annoyed.

"I don't mean to be a pest." I switched gears and continued in as un-pest-like a tone as I could manage. "Assuming Jemma's telling the truth, does she have any idea who could have broken in?"

"Most likely the guy who killed her sister. Jemma thinks he might have been looking for letters or a diary."

"That makes sense." *Just put a lid on it, Sharon. Quit asking questions. Quit....* "Why do you suppose she didn't level with Keziah's friends?"

"Maybe she suspects them too."

"Maybe I'll ask her myself."

"Maybe you should."

Ryan made a "T" with his hands. Time out.

Tom and I glared at each other in obstinate silence for a minute or two. Then I relented. I liked Tom, even if he was being bone-headed.

"Tom, I'm sorry. I didn't mean to put you on the defensive."

Tom rolled his shoulders and flexed his hands, which had been balled into fists. "I'm sorry too. I should have started off with the good news instead."

"Good news?"

"Phyllis and your friend Ms. Piffle gave us reason to pull in Bulldog."

CHAPTER 41

"That is good news! How did that come about?"

"Between the two of them, we finally had a picture to go on. Right or wrong, it was something we hadn't had before."

"What about pictures of Keziah?"

"Hers was all we had going for us at the beginning. Right after she disappeared. Or after we learned about her online connections. Okay, backtracking. After talking to the one guy who admitted meeting up with her, we showed her picture—and his—around every dive in town. The bartender at one place remembered them both. No one else had seen them together."

"I remember now. You weren't able to track down the other guys she contacted."

"Right. Some bartenders and some of the regulars thought her picture *might* look familiar. Some had a vague recollection of seeing her—never drinking anything but ginger ale of course." Tom rolled his eyes. "We let them know that wasn't our concern. We simply wanted to find Keziah and anyone she'd been seen with."

"But no one remembered anything else?"

"They weren't really paying attention—or said they weren't anyway. The few who acknowledged that *maybe* they'd seen her 'date' had even fuzzier descriptions. But once we had Bulldog's picture, once we had something concrete to show around, it jogged a few memories."

"So when did you locate the right place?"

"Saturday. Will and Roy nailed it Saturday. Bartender recognized the picture and even remembered seeing ol'

Bulldog with 'a young girl.' He couldn't swear it was Keziah. We brought Bulldog in today, and told him that both of them had been positively identified. He finally admitted he'd met Keziah at Rowdy's. But his story was that it was just a coincidence. He just 'happened to run into her there.' He denied knowing anything about emails. Which tells us he'd been pretty careful to keep from being traced."

"Wow. At least that's something. Could you pin down the date they were there?"

"That could be a problem. The bartender remembers it was Columbus Day, for some reason. Even Phyllis suggested Keziah got together with Bulldog before she started seeing this Franklin person."

"True. But I'd think the fact that Bulldog was with her at all could be pretty damning."

"Could be. Funny thing, he tried to turn the tables on us. Said some 'crazy woman' had been harassing him, and he knew his rights, yada yada yada. We said we'd look into it but needed more information."

"Oh dear, I hope you won't arrest Alvina."

"Nah. But it was hard to keep a straight face when we heard his side of the story. He said he'd gone to that play, 'just like any other law-abiding citizen.' Stepped outside for a smoke, and the crazy woman started yelling at him. Rather than make a scene and call attention to himself—wise move—he decided to hightail it as fast as he could, even though it meant missing the rest of the play. He's still a little pissed about that."

"Did he remember seeing her the day before at Ernie's?"

"Get this. He wasn't at Ernie's. He was in an A.A. meeting here in Alamo from noon to 2:00."

"Oh, for heaven's sake. So Mr. Nondescript really was a stranger."

"Looks like it."

"Then Saturday night was the first time he'd seen Alvina. Hmm. Strange he'd drive all the way to El Paso just to get away from her."

"His story was that he thought he could shake her for good in a big city. Which he did. Claimed he turned around, came back home, and went to bed. Interesting twist, his California car doesn't have a scratch on it."

"Talk about a strange turn of events. Two mysteries solved—or unsolved, depending on how you look at it. Bulldog and Mr. Nondescript aren't one and the same, and, apparently, neither of them had anything to do with Alvina's accident."

"Odd how a case of mistaken identity led us to connect Bulldog with Keziah. Ms. Piffle's report by itself seemed unrelated. Phyllis's description was second-hand, but when it matched Ms. Piffle's, well, there you have it."

"Speaking of Phyllis, we never had a chance to compare notes about your meeting with the kids the other day. I kinda wondered why you let Joel off the hook so quickly. I figured it had something to do with not wasting time listening to his lawyer-babble."

"That too. Remember, I wasn't expecting anyone but Dot to begin with. Then you told me all three girls would be here—which turned out to be helpful. But we'd already dealt with Joel and found out as much as we needed to. Except for the little fact that he might have been sweet on Keziah after all."

"Which he probably wouldn't have admitted without his so-called lawyer there. By the way, where did that come from?"

"The apple doesn't fall far, or however the saying goes. When we first questioned Joel—at his home—his dad was very cooperative. In fact he insisted that Joel cooperate too. You haven't met Deputy Lackmann—Pete Lackmann. He was there with us, and he knows more about computers than anyone on the planet. He unearthed all the info he needed from Joel's computer. Then before we left, Pete called Roy and had him access Keziah's Internet accounts from here, then make copies of everything."

"Something tells me her all accounts were cancelled shortly after that."

"Right. That very afternoon. Just to test Joel's reaction, Pete called him with some story about wanting to double-check something and suggesting we bring the computer back here. I think Joel's dad must have talked to his lawyer in the meantime, because 'suddenly' we couldn't talk to Joel anymore and couldn't do anything without a search warrant."

"I bet the little weasel forged the permission form I had them write up."

"I'm sure of it. He seems to be as good a forger as he is a computer whiz. I've filed all those forms. Never know when Joel's might come in handy."

"Do you consider him a suspect in Keziah's death?" Ryan asked.

"Good question. Considered it, though it seems unlikely. We think that phone call from Pete made Joel think he was a suspect, even though he wasn't at the time. We think that's what he's so uptight about. Being a suspect, not necessarily being a killer."

"So do you think he came down with the girls just to throw you off base?"

"Well put. I think he wanted to *appear* willing to help. Without actually being helpful."

"Devious little fart."

Tom laughed. "Good character analysis. Sure you and Sharon don't want to move out here and join us permanently?" Then his face turned grim. "We sure could use a break in this case."

CHAPTER 42

After leaving Tom's office, we went to the Teen Center, glad to find it still open during the Christmas break.

"Some kids need it more than ever," Brenda explained. "Especially if there's no one at home. Other kids are busy with family plans and whatnot. We wind up with some of the regulars plus several new faces. So the place is jumpin', as the kids would say."

Jumpin' indeed. The energy was palpable. Ryan joined Darryl and the carpenters and painters, who were busy putting finishing touches on some of the sets and starting work on others.

Inside the main building, kids were mostly milling around, though some had settled in with board or table games. Someone had brought in a DVD player. Others had pushed asides tables and chairs to make room for line dancing, which had drawn a number of followers.

"I wanted to tell you something privately," Brenda said as she led me into the office and closed the door. "Let's sit down, even though it'll only take a minute."

She was all smiles, so I figured whatever it was, it couldn't be bad.

"Dot came up and told me she felt 'sort of bad' if she'd been 'sort of rude' the other day," Brenda said, and we both chuckled.

"She said the girls thought Tom had sent me to spy," Brenda continued. "I answered with a half-truth, I guess you'd call it. I told them he hadn't 'sent' me, but didn't mention that he'd 'sort of' enlisted my help. I did say that everybody was worried and hoped to find out exactly how such a horrible thing could have happened."

"I'm glad she apologized. I like Dot, and her rudeness toward you had bothered me."

"I like her too. She can be headstrong and too much of an influence on her friends I think. But basically she's pretty grounded. Now she has a surprise for you. She didn't want me to tell you, so I'll bring the girls in here to tell you themselves."

Brenda was in and out of the office in less than two minutes, returning with Dot, Phyllis, and Wilma.

The girls had been next door, painting a surrey with a fringe on top. Not something you'd expect to cause overexertion. Yet they were so out-of-breath when they arrived, you'd think they'd been scaling the Rockies one by one.

Dot and Phyllis made no effort to tone down their excitement. Wilma tried to look bored, but didn't quite succeed.

"You'll never guess what happened, Ms. S.!" Dot said. Fortunately, since I was absolutely in the dark, she plunged right in with her news instead of waiting for me to make any wild guesses.

"We called Ms. Lathrop. Kezzie's art teacher."

"I was afraid she might not like us bothering her while she was on vacation," Phyllis chimed in. "But she was really nice."

"We asked her about looking at some of Kezzie's drawings and things," Dot continued, ignoring the interruption.

"She told us to meet her at the school," Phyllis said, determined to get a turn telling the good news.

"You wouldn't believe those pictures," Wilma added, a note of awe in her voice. "I never knew she had so much talent."

All three girls fell silent, perhaps struck with the realization that Keziah's talent had been quenched so abruptly.

"Well, now everyone has the opportunity to know," Brenda said softly. "Ms. Lathrop called me, and we arranged for the girls to bring Keziah's portfolio here. We're going to pick out some of the best of her paintings and hang them in the Teen Center."

"Except for one watercolor," Dot said. "You have to see it, Ms. S."

Brenda pulled the folio down from the top of the file cabinet and carefully spread the paintings a few at a time on her desk.

"Look at this one, Ms. S." Without touching it, Dot pointed almost reverently to a delicate watercolor in the middle of the group of paintings.

"It's Kezzie and Jemma," Phyllis added, in case I hadn't noticed that Keziah had labeled the picture "Me and My Sister," She had dated it "November 10"—just a few days before she'd gone missing, I realized with a start.

The portrait literally took my breath away. It was a close-up of the girls' faces, with their arms around each other's shoulders. In it, Keziah had managed to capture expressions of pure joy and love, somehow conveying both the fragility and the strength of their relationship.

Tears rolled down my cheeks, and I looked up to see the same response in Brenda.

"We want Jemma to have this," Wilma said quietly.

"Do you think she'll let us in?" Dot asked with an uncharacteristic lack of confidence.

"How about if we let Cindy—or Tom—be the one to go with you," Brenda said. "Let's at least ask them the best way to go about it."

"Can we call them right now?" Dot asked.

Brenda hesitated a moment, then, "Sure, why not?"

After leaving messages for each of the Alderetes, Brenda set aside the portrait, then spread out a few more paintings. "Now," she said, "let's decide which of these to put up in the Center."

I turned my attention back to the watercolor they planned to give Jemma. Something tickled the edge of my mind, but I couldn't bring it into focus.

It's significant echoed in my mind again. But I was still at a loss.

CHAPTER 43

"While we're waiting to hear back from Tom or Cindy, I have an idea," I said. "Let's take photographs of all Keziah's artwork. The photos can't replace the real thing, of course, but at least we'll have a good record."

"In case the real ones disappear again," Wilma said. She pressed her lips together in a tight line, and her thick glasses couldn't hide the tears forming in her eyes.

"Let's hope they don't," Brenda said. "But yes, it wouldn't hurt to have copies."

Dot's voice was gruff as she strained to sound matter-of-fact. "Who has a good digital camera?"

"We do," Brenda, Phyllis, and I said almost in unison.

"But none of them here, I bet. I can run over to The Lodge for ours and be back really quick. I'll bring my laptop too."

* * *

In the short time I was gone, Tom had returned Brenda's call. She explained the situation, telling him the girls wanted to surprise Jemma with the watercolor, but didn't know how to go about it without upsetting her again. Tom agreed to see if he could smooth the way.

So we were back to waiting once more. In the meantime, we were able to take the pictures we wanted and upload them to my laptop.

"Wow, they came out real sharp!" Dot said as we gathered around Brenda's desk and watched them appear on the computer screen. "I didn't think they would."

"I wasn't that sure myself," I said. "I'm glad it was worth the try."

"Me too," Brenda said. "How about if we upload them to my computer at home. Then I can email them to you girls and you'll each have copies of everything. Did Ms. Lathrop want the originals back—except for the one we're giving Jemma?"

"No," Phyllis answered. "She said she'd rather see them down here where everyone could enjoy them."

"Good. Since you all were such close friends of Keziah's, would you each like to pick one or two to keep for yourselves?"

"Yes," Dot said without hesitation. "I like the one of White Sands at sunset." She turned to Phyllis and Wilma. "Remember when we all went there together for a picnic?"

They nodded and mulled over several other paintings before settling on the ones they found especially meaningful. Wilma selected an oil depicting the Apple Festival at High Rolls, where they'd spent many a September day. Phyllis decided on a charcoal sketch of her family's St. Bernard.

"Now we need to choose the ones to give Jemma and the rest to keep here," Brenda said. "We can divide them however you'd like."

"Wow," Dot said again. "Ms. T., you're the best! You too, Ms. S. Thanks for—you know—taking the pictures."

"Well, I think it took all of us—and Ms. Lathrop—to bring this about," I said.

Wilma straightened up and glared at us over the rims of her glasses. "And now are we supposed to, like, forget Kezzie's dead?"

Dot glared back. "Are we supposed to forget she lived?"

Brenda intervened. "You'll be remembering both—her life and her death—and your feelings will be pretty raw for a while. So give each other a little space."

Phyllis stepped between her friends and put her arms around them. "Let's not fight."

The girls turned back to examining the originals, and I shut off the laptop, wrapped in my own mixed thoughts.

A few minutes later Tom called Brenda, and she relayed his message to us.

"Jemma's taking a few days off work, so she'll be home all day tomorrow. She'd like to see you all, but asked Tom to come too. He wondered if you could meet him at his office about 10:00 or so. Then you could go over to Jemma's together."

"Could you drive us down there?" Phyllis asked. "My mother volunteers at the Food Bank on Tuesday mornings."

"I'd like to, but I'm supposed to be here all day."

"What about you?" Dot asked me.

"No problem. But I still need permission from your folks."

Dot grinned. "No problem."

CHAPTER 44

Ryan, figuring our entourage was already large enough, decided to stay in Cloudcroft and work with Darryl on the lighting for the play. So I drove the girls to Tom's office in Alamogordo, watercolor in hand.

Rather, watercolor in frame. Dot had called Keziah's art teacher again, this time to explain what they had in mind. Ms. Lathrop was not only delighted that they planned to give Jemma the picture of the two sisters, but offered to frame it for them.

"She's so nice," Phyllis said. "By the time we got home from the Teen Center, it was, like, too late to find a place in town to do it, and even if we had, they probably couldn't have gotten it back to us right away."

I admired Ms. Lathrop's artistic sense in more ways than one. I've seen frames that overpower the picture they're framing. But this one was simply a thin tubular band surrounding a narrow mat, each in a shade of aqua that brought out the colors in the painting.

* * *

Dressed casually—in jeans, a western shirt, and cowboy boots—instead of in uniform, Tom looked younger than his 26 years. If he had any misgivings about the upcoming visit with Jemma, it didn't show.

"Do you want to see Kezzie's picture now, or wait till we get to Jemma's," Dot asked, unable to contain her eagerness.

He grinned. "You mean I get a preview?"

"Yeah, if you want to," Wilma said.

"I'd like that. Then the surprise can be for Jemma alone."

"Let me," Phyllis said. She laid the watercolor on Tom's desk and unwrapped it carefully. Then the girls all watched Tom for his reaction.

He stared at the painting for a few moments without saying anything. Then he spoke in a husky voice, "No wonder...."

"Do you think Jemma will like it? I mean, do you think she'll want to keep it?" Phyllis asked. Her anxiety spoke for all the girls, their tension doing battle with their excitement.

In that moment, I think Tom realized that, whichever version of Keziah's missing belongings was true, the girls' encounter with Jemma had unnerved them.

"She'll like it, I promise," he assured them. Then he turned to me. "Why don't you leave your car here, and I'll drive us to Jemma's."

Tom's Mazda wasn't new, but it was sporty enough to impress the girls. Jemma's place was less than a mile away, so we arrived within minutes. It was a small house that reminded me of a story-book cottage with a little picket fence around it. Set on a large lot, it was well away from the main house. A long driveway leading to a two-car garage served both houses.

Apparently other neighbors' vehicles had outnumbered their respective garages, since so many cars were parked on both sides of the street. Tom found a place on a side street, and we walked from there up the driveway to reach Jemma's. She was watching for us out the picture window and opened the door before we even rang the bell. She hugged Tom and greeted the rest of us pleasantly, though with some reserve.

The living room was attractive, though furnished with only a couch, two armchairs, and a coffee table. Curtains along the window and a round rug in the middle of the room softened the sparseness. Jemma must have liked the same shades of aqua and turquoise that Keziah liked, since those were the colors she'd chosen to decorate the room.

A mouthwatering aroma filled the air—ginger, cinnamon, and other spices I couldn't pin down.

"I invited Elise," Jemma said, lifting her chin in a gesture that discouraged questions or comments. "She thought you'd need refreshments, so she's busy making gingerbread."

"That sounds good," I said, clever conversationalist that I am.

Jemma finally noticed that we were still standing, still wearing our coats. She motioned toward the couch and chairs. "Find someplace to sit. Uh. Would you like me to take your wraps?"

"Sure." Tom took off his coat. "I'll help." He held out his hands for our coats, dividing them between himself and Jemma.

"We'll put them on the bed, if that's okay," she said. She didn't wait for us to answer, but she and Tom disappeared momentarily into a room connected to the living room. I was curious to see the rest of the house, but Jemma didn't seem the sort to offer a tour.

The girls sat on the couch, somewhat gingerly, still unsure of their welcome, and I chose one of the armchairs. Jemma and Tom rejoined us, Tom toting some folding chairs he'd pulled from the hall closet.

Another door led into the kitchen, where I could see someone—probably Elise—rinsing her hands at the sink. A few moments later she entered the living room, drying her hands with a towel.

Tall, thirtyish, with straight blond hair and a few freckles sprinkled across her pale skin, she seemed rather plain at first. But there was a vibrancy about her that dispelled that initial impression, and I noticed only her sparkling blue eyes and generous smile instead. She introduced herself and immediately made us feel at home.

"I just took a loaf of gingerbread out of the oven," she said. "There's nothing like warm gingerbread with a cold glass of milk." She smiled at the girls. "But that can wait. I don't want to interrupt your plans."

Encouraged by Elise's kindness. Dot laid the painting, still wrapped, on the coffee table.

Tom nudged Jemma. "Come see what they've brought."

Jemma shrugged, then sat cross-legged on the floor in front of the coffee table.

Wilma stood by silently, her eyes more solemn than ever behind her thick glasses.

"I hope you'll like it," Phyllis said shyly as she unwrapped it.

Jemma stared, stunned, for a long moment, then buried her face in her hands and began sobbing, her shoulders shaking as she rocked back and forth.

"It's about time," Elise said softly. "About time she cried."

Elise bent over the painting to see it for herself and took in a quick breath. "Look at that! How she loved you, Jem. I told you so."

Elise knelt beside Jemma and laid her arm lightly on her shoulder. Jemma's crying subsided, and Elise found her a tissue. By now the girls were teary-eyed themselves. Even

Tom and I were not immune, and the Kleenex box was passed around.

"Thank you," Jemma said hoarsely. "All of you. I don't know what else to say."

Jemma stood and surprised me by giving us all hugs—brief but heartfelt.

"Do you know when Kezzie painted this?" she asked.

"There's a date at the bottom of the picture," Dot said.

Jemma looked at it more closely. "Not long after Halloween. That figures. I got really good tips that night—Halloween night. So the next day, I treated us to a trip to a beauty salon. We got the works—haircut, manicure, pedicure."

Her voice became wistful. "We had so much fun that day.... We even went to one of those booths in the mall where you can take your own picture. We did several poses, some goofy, some not. Kezzie wanted to keep them, but I didn't know she planned to use them."

Phyllis looked at the picture again. "I really liked Kezzie's hair that way. Kinda short, but not too short. A little curly. Just, like, soft around her face."

And that's when it struck me. *That* was the significant detail that had escaped me earlier.

CHAPTER 45

Elise reminded us to come get some gingerbread while it was still warm. We followed her out to the kitchen, a cheerful room with yellow walls adorned by curtains and tablecloth patterned with sunflowers.

"I like to think of summer things on days when it's cold outside," Elise explained. "Even though it's never as cold here as in the mountains. And Jemma told me —even though I don't live here—since I'm the one who spends more time in the kitchen, I could fix it up any way I liked."

The fragrance of gingerbread that permeated the home had whetted all our appetites. Tom once again brought extra folding chairs, and we quickly seated ourselves around the table. Elise served generous slices of the treat, along with milk or coffee.

While I enjoyed the refreshments, I could hardly wait to talk with Tom and wondered how to go about it without spoiling the happy atmosphere.

I caught his eye across the table and felt in a flash that we were on the same wavelength. Well, he was the detective; I'd wait for him to bring up the subject.

The girls offered to help Elise clean up, but she shooed all of us out of the kitchen. "Next time," she said, as we re-entered the living room.

"If you always cook like that," Tom said, "'next time' will be very soon."

Elise laughed and tweaked his ear. "I hope so."

"Right now we need to get going."

Jemma turned toward the bedroom. "I'll get your coats."

"Wait a minute," Tom said. "I need to ask you something first. Do you have any of those pictures you and your sister took at the mall?"

She stopped, then looked back at him. "No, she kept all of them. She might have brought them to her art class. If she took them home...." Jemma's eyes hardened. "They're gone."

"We took photos of all her paintings," I said. "We can make a copy of this one and crop it."

"Why? What are you talking about?"

Tom and I locked eyes again, then he turned his attention back to Jemma. "We used the wrong picture in the flyers."

"It was all I had," Jemma said defensively.

Tom reached for her hand. "I'm not blaming you. I think people who knew her recognized her from the flyers. Recognized her with her hair pulled back. But...other people...might have seen her with curly hair instead. We'd like to ask around again."

"Oh.... Of course. I wasn't thinking."

"Don't worry about it. What *you* need to do is find a place to hang Keziah's gift."

Worry lines creased her forehead. "I couldn't bear for it to get stolen. Would you keep it for me, Tom, until—until it's safe again?"

"If that's what you want."

A grim look crossed Elise's face. "That's a good idea. I'm not sure it would be safe with me either."

Dot, Wilma, and Phyllis looked at one another, puzzled and ill-at-ease again.

Jemma faced them. "I lied to you the other day. It was easier. I didn't want to explain."

Dot nodded, still puzzled.

Tom stepped in. "Someone broke into Jemma's house. It was hard to deal with on top of everything else."

Phyllis gasped. "Oh, that's awful!"

Jemma's expression softened. "Yes, it is. But Sheriff Gibson is working on it, and they have some good leads."

Another lie. I wondered if I was overly suspicious or overly imaginative. We'll see if Tom *really* considers me part of the team.

* * *

Whispers punctuated by occasional chattering emanated from the back seat on the drive back. Right before we reached Tom's office, Dot leaned forward and tapped him on the shoulder.

"Sgt. Tom, do you think Jemma's on drugs?"

I caught a glimpse of him flexing his fingers and glancing in the rear-view mirror.

"No. Do you think she is?"

"I don't know. Well, it's hard to know how she'll react to anything. Like, she seems happy one minute and then mad for no reason."

"She's been under quite a strain."

"And we don't think she really felt bad about lying to us."

Tom pulled into his parking space. "Come on inside. Maybe we need to iron this out."

"What time is it?" Phyllis asked. "I'm supposed to call my mom when we're ready to leave. She said she could pick us up."

"Why don't you give her a ring now?" I suggested. "That should give us plenty of time before she gets here."

Phyllis nodded, flipped open her cell phone, and made the call from the parking lot. Tom took the painting into his office while the rest of us filed into the conference room, shed our coats, and settled ourselves in the navy-blue chairs.

Tom joined us, sat down and leaned forward, arms folded on the table. The girls waited for him to take the lead.

"Okay, here goes. I've known Jemma a long time, and she's always been a bunch of contradictions. So I won't even try to explain why she acts the way she does. But I do know she's anti-drug down to the core."

"And that might be part of her problem," I said. "She's probably afraid of getting addicted to over-the-counter meds. Something like a sleeping pill once in a while might help."

Dot and Wilma looked skeptical, but Phyllis nodded in agreement. "My mom's like that. She doesn't even like to take aspirin."

Impatiently, Dot waved away Phyllis's mother and her aversion to medicine. "I want to know about Jemma. Do you think she really wanted the picture, or is it just something else she's gonna get rid of?"

For once, Tom's poker face slipped, and he looked as shocked as I felt, his expression registering a mixture of surprise, sadness, and anger. "How could you even think that?"

"Think a minute, Dot," I said. "If she didn't want the picture, she could have just said 'thank you,' and waited for us to leave. I'm as confused as you about why she lied earlier. But one thing she didn't lie about, that picture meant a lot to her. She wants to keep it, and she wants it to be safe."

"I'm sorry we thought she was on drugs," Wilma mumbled.

"It's easy to misinterpret things. I'm just glad we had a chance to talk it out."

The mood lightened, and conversation turned to gingerbread and the pleasant aspects of our visit while the girls waited for Charlene.

My mind drifted as I came to my own conclusions about Jemma's lies and her odd behavior.

CHAPTER 46

"I'm guessing," I said, "since you're not in uniform, today's your day off."

Tom grinned. "You guessed right. But I need to get Jemma's painting stashed away—after making a photocopy of Keziah's picture. In fact, now that we have something new to go on, I'd like to get started on the investigation again."

Charlene had picked up the girls, and I had looked forward to a chance to brainstorm with Tom, but I also understood how impatient he was to move ahead. While he made photocopies, I debated with myself about impinging on his free time. My own time was running short; we were due to go home day after tomorrow.

My indecision was cut short by a call from Jemma to Tom. I heard him say, "Mm-hmm, mm-hmm," a few times before he handed the phone to me.

Jemma's voice had that brittle quality I'd begun to associate with her. Still, there was a note of something else—anxiety? trepidation? Her words came out in a rush, as if she wanted to say what she had to say before losing her nerve.

"Sharon, could you come over? If you have time? Tom tells me you're very perceptive—and nice—and I need to talk to someone who doesn't know me."

"Sure." I looked at my watch. Ryan wasn't expecting me anytime soon, so I easily had the rest of the afternoon. "Would you like me to come now?"

"Yes." She let out a long breath. "Before I change my mind."

"I'll be there pretty quick. Give me about fifteen minutes."

She hung up without another word. I knew I'd go there whether she changed her mind or not. Tom looked at me quizzically, and I chose to interpret that to mean he'd be delighted to have me interrupt him.

I told him about Jemma's request, then said I'd like to ask him some questions before going over there, if he didn't mind. "I'm not sure what I'm getting into. Is there something about looking and leaping that I've ignored?"

Tom pulled his chair out from behind his desk, and motioned for me to sit across from him. He sat down, rested one booted foot on the opposite knee, folded his hands behind his head, and looked at me in amusement. "Ask away."

"For starters, has Jemma ever gone for counseling?"

He frowned. "She tried once. Probably a bad match with that particular therapist. Jemma reaches a certain point talking about her family life and then she shuts down. I think the therapist suggested anti-depressants, and Jemma was outta there."

"Okay. It helps to know what not to suggest."

"There's something else, isn't there."

"You're perceptive too. Like Ryan. If he was here, he'd say he could see the wheels turning in my brain. Anyway, I wish I could see Jemma's wheels. I think she knows who broke into her house, and she wasn't ready to deal with it when the girls showed up. So she made up the first excuse that came to mind."

"I'm with you."

"Do you think she's trying to protect someone? The only person I can think of is Elise, and that seems unlikely."

"I don't know. Unless Elise thought it would help her to 'move on.'"

"Maybe there's a little jealousy there," I said. "If Jemma's so focused on Keziah, when does she have time for Elise?"

"Maybe Elise isn't all she seems to be. Maybe all that hospitality stuff is just an act."

I rubbed my temples with my fingertips. "Could be, but I'd really hate to think that. She seems so warm and...nurturing. I felt she was—is—good for Jemma."

"I know. I like Elise too. But—*something* doesn't add up."

"You're right. One more thing, would you mind if I look up something online before I get going?"

"Not at all. Let me get the computer fired up."

He pulled his chair behind the desk again, sat down, and got started. "A little slow. Taxpayer dollars at work."

I stood behind him and looked over his shoulder. While we watched icons sluggishly marching into place. I told Tom about the online search I'd started for Keziah after I'd looked up local predators. "I know it sounds odd." I could feel my face reddening. "That so-called warning out of the blue. So I thought if I tried again in broad daylight, with someone else there, I wouldn't get spooked again."

"Here you are," he said, getting up so I could sit at the computer.

I typed in Keziah's name and held my breath. The first thing that showed up was a newspaper article about her death. Something about dedicated police work. No mention of skiers—or even snowmobilers. Memorial services pending. No mention of mortuary or survivors. I wondered if the "dedicated police work" included keeping details to a minimum.

I felt my skin prickle when I clicked on the next item. The headline read, "Local Teen Missing." I skimmed through the article without noticing anything alarming. Good.

I read through it more carefully, but didn't see any details that jumped out at me. In summary it stated that Keziah had been missing for several days. Her disappearance was reported by her sister, Jemma Porter. The parents, Athaliah and Hezekiah Porter, were unavailable for comment.

The tingling sensation intensified, but I still didn't know why.

CHAPTER 47

By the time I got to Jemma's, I was feeling fatalistic. If she wanted to see me, fine. If she'd changed her mind, that was fine too.

She was looking for me out the window. I smiled and waved, then ambled up the steps to her porch. No point in appearing overeager. She opened the door, invited me in, and locked the door behind us.

"I'm not locking you in," she said. "Just keeping intruders out."

As usual, she was guarded, and I wondered how I could possibly help. I felt like shouting at her to call a professional, someone skilled in dealing with troubled people. At the same time, I knew from experience that a sympathetic ear could break barriers. I said a quick prayer that we'd connect with each other.

"Would you like coffee?" she asked.

Not especially, but maybe a social setting would ease Jemma into revealing what was really bothering her. "Sure," I said. "Coffee sounds good."

I followed her into the kitchen and sat at the table.

"Do you want cream? Sugar?"

"No sugar. Cream or the powdery stuff."

She brought out Coffeemate and sat opposite me. We both added the creamer, stirred, and talked about coffee—brewed vs. instant—for a minute or two.

I wasn't surprised that Jemma was too impatient to linger over small talk for very long.

"It was my mother who let herself in and emptied Kezzie's room," she blurted out.

I was taken aback. "Oh? How did you find out?"

"The Nelsons, the people who own this place and live in the main house, they saw her coming and going but assumed she had permission, since they knew who she was."

"I thought you kept the door locked."

"I always do if the Nelsons aren't home, but I don't—didn't used to—worry if they were there. Besides I thought I was making a quick trip to Lowe's. Spent more time than I meant to."

"Did you have the locks changed?"

She shook her head. "I didn't see any need to. Since she didn't actually break in."

"I see."

"There's more. The Witch had the gall to leave me a note." Pain filled Jemma's eyes. "She wanted to obliterate every shred of evidence that Kezzie ever existed."

My stomach did a flip-flop. "That's disturbing."

"It's monstrous."

I nodded.

"What's even worse," she said softly, "I wanted to get rid of Kezzie's things myself, and I'd even started packing them up."

"But for different reasons, right?"

She closed her eyes for a moment, then faced me again. "Yes. Mixed-up reasons. I missed her, and seeing her things was a constant reminder." Her voice turned harsh. "I was angry too."

"Jemma, it's not unusual to feel that way. To act that way."

"I was angry because I couldn't control her. I think I'm turning into a control-freak. A crazy control-freak!" Jemma became even more strident. "I'm going crazy. Like my mother. I think I inherited some bad gene of hers. Like a cancer!"

My mouth went dry as I searched for something to say. "Jemma, maybe your mother's problem isn't hereditary. Maybe there was some traumatic event you don't even know about."

Jemma stared at me for a moment in that disconcerting way she had.

"Maybe that car accident she was in caused a brain injury," I plowed on. "I know you were too young to analyze a personality change. But try to remember, was there a difference in your mother's behavior before and after the accident?"

Jemma continued staring, but this time it was directed toward some distant space beyond me, as if she was trying to form a picture in her mind of their life back then.

"They were never very demonstrative—my parents. But they weren't cruel. Just absent emotionally."

I felt a pang of recognition and gripped the edge of the table to keep my own emotions at bay. *This isn't about* your *mother, Sharon. This isn't about you*, I reminded myself.

Lost in her own thoughts, Jemma didn't notice my momentary stiffness. "After the accident, my grandmother stayed with us for a while. I don't know how long. Six weeks or six months. I had no concept of time, and my memory's pretty dim anyway."

"What was your grandmother like?"

Jemma's voice softened. "She was sweet. Y'know, maybe that maternal gene skips every other generation. I must have gotten it from my grandmother. Even though I don't intend to have children. But I loved Kezzie from the first moment I held her. I thought she was the prettiest little thing I'd ever seen. And I've always felt protective toward her."

"See? You inherited some good genes after all."

"I hope so. And I think you're right about my mother changing about then. I never put two and two together. I just thought she was angry because my grandmother went back home and she was left with so much work to do alone. She told us that often enough. About how we caused her such hard work. Caused her so much misery. She blamed Dad for their accident. Whether he was actually at fault or not, I don't know. He'd yell that he wasn't. Eventually he turned surly and quit arguing with her, and that just fueled her anger."

"How about you? You and Keziah?"

Jemma was silent for a while before whispering, "Sometimes she told us she wished we'd never been born."

Tears came to my eyes. I couldn't begin to grasp what that could do to a child's psyche. A maternal gene seemed to have skipped my mother too, but I believe she tried her best—in her own way. Her failings paled compared to Mrs. Porter's.

"I think it's amazing you survived," I said.

"I was lucky. School was my refuge. I had wonderful teachers—something else I didn't analyze at the time. Thank goodness the home-school thing flopped. For me. Kezzie was always more compliant, and I didn't think of the consequences of her having to stay at home a few more years. That's about the time my mother got involved in this religious cult. If her brain wasn't screwed up before, it sure went to hell after that."

"Well, whenever and however, it seems pretty clear to me it wasn't a genetic disorder." *For what my pseudo-medical opinion is worth.* "Something else, Jemma. There's nothing abnormal about wanting to be in control. It's just when—" *when control gets out of control. There has to be a better way to word this.* "—when taking charge gets out of hand that it needs to be dealt with."

"I'll have to think about that."

"Okay, think about this too. This is another major difference between you and your mother. You don't want to be manipulative. From what I understand, your mother has no qualms about it."

"That's what Elise says. That I have a conscience and The Witch doesn't."

"Elise sounds very wise."

Jemma covered her face with her hands and began crying. "I never cry. And now I've cried twice in one day."

"Count it a good day." I walked around the table, put my arm around her shoulders and gave her a quick hug.

We had no way of knowing the good day would turn upside-down in a matter of minutes.

CHAPTER 48

Jemma stood, pulled a few tissues from the Kleenex box, and blew her nose. "I'll be okay now."

"You're sure?"

"Yeah. I think I'll go to Walmart and pick up some twinkle lights or something. The Witch said Christmas was a pagan holiday, so we never had any decorations at home. This year will really be different. I don't care so much for myself, but Elise goes in for the whole thing—the manger, the carols, the color, the lights, everything."

"I'm with Elise. I like it all too."

Jemma smiled. "Maybe I can surprise her. She'll be back later on. She's an RN for a doctor in our building—that's how I met her. She took the morning off but needed to work this afternoon."

"Good. I'm glad you have something to look forward to."

As Jemma walked me to the door, we heard footsteps coming up the steps to the porch.

"Who could that be? The UPS guy? I wasn't expecting anything," Jemma mused, stopping to pull the curtain back and peer out the picture window.

Neither of us could see anyone from where we stood, but I felt that sudden inner chill.

"Don't open the door."

We stood immobilized, listening to the scratchy sound a key makes in a lock.

"Are the Nelsons home?" I whispered. "Do they have a key."

She shook her head.

Without giving it conscious thought, I sprang to one of the armchairs and began shoving it against the door. Just as quickly, Jemma joined me. Together we almost had the door blocked against a resistant push from the other side before it moved an inch or two.

"Jemma. Let me in."

"Go away, Ma!"

The pressure on the door stopped, and we heard light footsteps, as if the woman was tip-toeing away.

"Is there another way in?" I asked.

"The back door. Quick! Dammit—she must have Kezzie's key," Jemma muttered as we hurried to the kitchen. "After saying she'd thrown everything away."

We were shoving the kitchen table toward the back door when Mrs. Porter slipped in ahead of us, her eyes glittering with triumph.

For a moment I was so consumed by that unearthly cold I thought I'd either pass out or throw up. *Danger. Danger to Jemma all along.*

"Where did you come from?" Mrs. Porter asked me. "I didn't see any strange cars out front."

Shivering, I cleared my throat and lied. "I walked." She didn't need to know I'd parked on a side street. Where she'd probably had to park too. "Um. We were just on our way to Walmart. Maybe you can come back later," I added, as if I was in charge.

"I don't think so. Jemma's not going anywhere. Not until she repents of her sins."

She smiled, or at least stretched her lips in a facsimile of a smile. It crossed my mind that she might have done something to Jemma's car. She clutched her purse to her chest, making me wonder what was inside. Poison? Her favorite gun? A knife?

The good news was that she seemed to expect Jemma to be alone. I took a few leaden steps away from Jemma, hoping it would make it harder to keep both of us in focus. Hoping I was doing the right thing. Divide and unconquer was my motto for the time being.

The woman turned to Jemma but pointed a bony finger at me. "Is this the floozy you've taken up with?"

Floozy? Despite the chill, I almost laughed. Floozy! An old-fashioned word I'd expect someone my grandmother's age to use. And certainly a tame word coming from Mrs. Porter.

My grandmother. Her sweet face came clearly to mind. "Gram, pray for me," I pleaded silently. I took a deep breath and the chill subsided.

"She's a friend," Jemma answered, her voice strained.

"That's not what I'd call it," Mrs. Porter spat out. "An abomination, that's what it is. Unnatural."

The lawyer in me popped out before I had time to think about it. "Unnatural? Loving someone is unnatural? As opposed to tormenting your children?"

Her eyes drilled into mine, so I gazed at a spot over her left shoulder. Irrelevant thoughts came to mind. She looked and acted like my idea of an old crone. A picture out of one of those nightmarish storybooks supposedly written for children. A crone maybe, but she couldn't be that old. Maybe even my age. After all, I was—theoretically—old enough to be Jemma's mother.

"Whores of Satan, all of you. Keziah was the worst. She refused to repent."

I glanced over at Jemma, dismayed to see that her skin had taken on a pale greenish tinge.

A look of horror filled her face as she stared at her mother. "You killed her, didn't you!"

"She had it coming," Mrs. Porter snapped.

"No! No, no, no, no, no!" Jemma's voice rose in a primitive wail.

I forgot my earlier resolution and closed the distance between us. I didn't know if we'd have time to make it to the bathroom, so guided her to the kitchen sink, keeping my arm around her waist. She gripped the edge of the sink, leaned over, and vomited.

When the retching stopped, I turned on the faucet and filled a small glass with water. "Don't drink this, just rinse your mouth out," I ordered. Afterwards I ran water in the sink. Next I pulled a paper towel from the roller, held it under the faucet till it was fairly drenched, then wiped Jemma's face.

"Let's sit down," I said, as if we were the only two people in the house and her mother an insignificant cardboard figure on the sidelines. Jemma and I sat side by side on the couch while I held her clammy hand—probably contributing to her mother's view of our "depravity."

"And you've brought it on yourselves," Mrs. Porter rasped.

CHAPTER 49

"How could you?" Jemma moaned.

Mrs. Porter had followed us into the living room, still grasping her handbag, and seated herself on the armchair opposite us—the one not propped against the door. "It's easier than you'd think," she answered Jemma with a sly grin. "Smothering someone isn't that hard."

"I didn't mean it that way. I meant...never mind."

I knew what Jemma meant, but I couldn't help wondering about the logistics. The timeline puzzled me. Keziah had been missing several weeks before we found her. And the autopsy showed she'd been alive up until a day or two before that.

"Was she at your house all along? While everyone thought she was missing? While everyone was searching?" I wanted to know; at the same time, I was almost afraid to hear what she might say.

"That Alderete kid thinks he's so smart. But he and that sheriff are no match for Athaliah Porter." She cackled, her eyes too opaque to mirror her supposed merriment.

Typical of smug and arrogant people, Mrs. Porter welcomed the chance to show how clever she'd been. Fine with me. It might buy us time against whatever malice she planned next.

"I listen to the radio," she said. "I knew Jemma had told them Keziah was missing. I knew they'd come up to our place to ask questions. You can hear people coming up that rocky road a mile away. So I put her in Brutus's house."

"Brutus?" I asked.

"That's our Doberman," Jemma murmured.

"Keziah was shut up with your Doberman?" Disbelief mingled with horror.

"He wouldn't hurt Kezzie," Jemma said, "but still—what a horrible cramped place...what a cruel thing...."

"Keziah just stayed there—without making a sound?" I asked, incredulous.

Tom had told me they had to tie the dog up. How the Porters must have gloated that Brutus was standing right outside the place they'd hidden Keziah, snarling and straining against his leash. Who would have thought to search there?

"You drugged her first, didn't you, Ma," Jemma said. "That stuff Dad takes for his pain. You gave it to us before when we tried to leave. Only we caught on. How did you fool Kezzie this time?"

Mrs. Porter's face took on a crafty look. "Something different the doctor gave him. It doesn't taste so bad."

"How long was she there?" Jemma asked.

"Not long. The hotshots from the sheriff's office didn't stay long."

"No, I didn't mean that. I meant—how long had she been home...or what passes for home," she added under her breath.

Mrs. Porter's face distorted with anger. "Don't sass me!"

Jemma swallowed hard. "Sorry."

"She was a schemer, just like you. But I found out what she was up to, what a slut she was. When she was still going to school like she was supposed to, she guarded that cell phone with her life. Slept with it under her pillow. As if I wouldn't notice."

"So once again you gave her some of Dad's meds." Jemma's voice was dull, toneless.

Mrs. Porter, on the other hand, was lost in self-congratulation. "She didn't even taste it. Barely had time to put on her nightgown before she was out like a light. I slid that phone out with no trouble at all. I figured she'd have an easy password. She wasn't real bright, used her birthday."

Mrs. Porter gave Jemma another of her twisted self-satisfied smiles. "I bet you forgot you taught me all about cell phones. Back when I had to pick up Keziah after school. Not that I ever used the phone you gave me—"

"So, once you had her password," Jemma interrupted, a tremor in her voice belying her bravado, "did you call all her friends?"

I cringed at the sarcasm, expecting another angry outburst from her mother. But Mrs. Porter either didn't notice or didn't care.

"I checked her messages. There weren't that many calls, but lots of texts. Enough to find out she was planning to meet one of Satan's own in a couple of days. I put the phone back under her pillow, and she never knew."

I could feel Jemma shaking and wondered if she was going into shock. I reached back and pulled a turquoise and cream-colored afghan from across the back of the couch, then wrapped it around her shoulders.

Mrs. Porter continued in her single-minded way. "I didn't let on. The next morning she went to school as usual. You picked her up afterwards like you always do on Fridays. I drove into town and parked outside Rowdy's Bar and waited. When they got there—Keziah and the scum she was with—I stopped them cold and made her come back home with me. He took off, like the coward he was."

"Why didn't you let me know?" Jemma asked, her voice trembling. "Why did you let people think she'd gone missing?"

"They wouldn't let me keep her at home. The school. CYFD. They think they're in charge of my family. *My* family. Mine. Instruments of the devil, that's what they are. Just like the sheriff and his mob. Well, I told you how I handled them when they barged into my house, acting so high and mighty."

I didn't think Will and Tom constituted a mob, but that was the least of her delusions.

"That girl had to be punished. She'd used her cell phone for evil purposes, so I destroyed it. I gave her plenty of time, gave her every chance, but she just got more defiant. She said she'd rather be dead, so I handed her over to Satan."

Jemma slid to the other end of the couch and lay down on her side, pulling her knees up to her chest and staring into space. If she really was going into shock, she needed more help than I could give her. I tucked the afghan around her, wishing I could think of something heroic to do.

CHAPTER 50

What did Mrs. Porter have in mind for Jemma? For me? Drugging Keziah would have made it easy to tie her wrists behind her back, rendering her unable to struggle. Surely she hadn't planned to waltz into the house and smother Jemma too.

Right now the woman seemed content to gloat over her cleverness. I had mixed feelings about hearing any more of her grisly recital, yet I was as puzzled as I was repulsed. Plus, it seemed a good idea to keep her talking.

"Why did you take Keziah up to the mountain?"

"Well, I couldn't bury her on our property. Not with the authorities nosing around. And I couldn't very well bury her in the churchyard, now could I."

"Did you think no one would find her?"

"Oh, I knew they'd find her sooner or later. I thought it would be later, but it didn't really matter. She liked to hike, so I dressed her up real warm. Figured it would look like she'd been hiking and lost her way."

You really are *delusional, aren't you.*

Mrs. Porter hugged her purse again. What was in it? Tom said she enjoyed waving a gun around. I thought he'd called it a shotgun, but that didn't mean she didn't have some kind of handgun as well.

Maybe I could lull her into dropping her guard, at least long enough for me to slam into her and wrestle her purse from her before she had a chance to open it.

And right now, I wasn't thinking clearly myself. Maybe I was just as delusional. In fact, another image was forming.

Was it all in my mind, or had Elise just floated inside the back door and skirted the table we hadn't quite managed to push against it?

When her eyes met mine, she put her finger to her lips and continued gliding into the living room.

I looked down at my hands, afraid if I looked anyplace else, my face would give me away. Mrs. Porter continued babbling about something, but my ears were on overload.

Elise continued her stealthy move toward Mrs. Porter, who was suddenly aware that someone was right behind her. When she turned to look over her shoulder, Elise struck her in the temple with the only heavy object she had at hand—a thick medical book she'd brought home for research.

Without giving Mrs. Porter time to react, Elise struck her a couple more times till she crumpled to the floor. I grabbed her purse, not that she was in any condition to notice, and opened it to find a small-caliber Beretta.

I stood where I'd be blocking Jemma's view, then took the gun out, flicked off the safety, and pointed it at Mrs. Porter, praying I wouldn't have to use it. The purse fell to the floor.

"Your hands are shaking," Elise said, reaching for the gun. "Go look in Jemma's dresser drawer and find some socks, tee-shirts, anything we can use to tie up Mrs. Porter till she comes to again. I have no idea where Jemma keeps rope, if she even has any."

I didn't have to be told twice. I handed Elise the gun, then went into Jemma's bedroom. For a moment, but only a moment, I hesitated about rummaging through her personal things. Her winter socks seemed too bulky for making knots, so I picked out a few tee-shirts instead.

The gun traded hands again. I wasn't any less shaky, but it seemed less likely that we'd need it. With a nurse's skill, Elise wrapped and tied the shirts around Mrs. Porter's hands and feet. The woman made no signs of moving, and I wondered if the blows to her temple had been too severe. Not that I would have minded, but I didn't want Elise to face the consequences.

While Elise turned her attention to Jemma, I called 911, Ryan, and Tom Alderete in that order. I left a message for Ryan to meet us at the hospital, hoping we'd be there by the time he got to Alamogordo, telling him I was okay and that I'd explain later.

My message to Tom simply said, "Call back when you can."

"While we're waiting for the medics, I'm going to fix some hot tea," I told Elise.

"Good idea. You look pretty drained."

"May I fix you a cup?"

"Maybe later. No. Go ahead now. It might be good for both our nerves. I'm starting to feel a little unsteady myself."

I picked up Mrs. Porter's purse and slipped the Beretta inside. Then I headed for the kitchen and left the purse on the counter. The authorities could pick it up later and decide how to handle it.

Once the tea was brewed, I took our cups into the living room, setting them on the end table. Elise was massaging Jemma's hands and talking softly to her. I was glad to see that Jemma was conscious and no longer locked in a fetal position but lying on her back, her legs elevated. Her color had come back, and her breathing was even.

I pushed the armchair back in place and sat in it, then took a few soothing sips of tea. "Elise, how did you know

Jemma was in danger?" I asked, keeping my voice low to match hers.

"Tom called me." She hesitated. "He's probably on the way here now."

Hearing sirens, I said, "It looks like the EMTs are here too, thank goodness!"

Tea forgotten, I opened the door; then Elise and I stepped aside while the medical team went to work.

I tried to reach Tom again, leaving a different message this time, asking him to meet us at the hospital.

CHAPTER 51

Once the ambulance hauled Mrs. Porter away, I lost track of it for the time being. Elise drove Jemma to the hospital, then stayed with her in the examining room. I followed them as far as the ER, then parked in the visitor parking lot.

Not thinking clearly when I left a message for Ryan to meet us here, I'd forgotten that I was driving our only car. Fortunately Darryl offered his car without a moment's hesitation when Ryan relayed my message.

He had reached the ER before the rest of us, and I practically flung myself into his arms the moment I saw him.

"Dammit, Sharon," he said, his embrace belying his gruffness. "You have a bad habit of telling me to meet you at the hospital and not to worry."

"Only one other time I did that. And that was a long time ago. Well, kind of long. I wouldn't call that a habit."

His fingers traced the tears on my face. "Okay, now tell me."

Thanks to Elise's intervention, Ryan and I were able to sit in the privacy of a small conference room next to the ER waiting room. I explained about Mrs. Porter's worming her way into Jemma's home, then told him the details of the woman's confession, about the way Jemma had fallen apart, and how Elise had rescued us.

"Good lord, Sharon. And you tell me not to worry?"

"I know. Saying it out loud makes it sound even more surreal."

Less than a minute later, Tom joined us and I explained it all again.

"Tom, Elise said you'd warned her that Jemma was in danger," I said. "How could you know?"

"I guess it's my turn. I've said before how one link leads to another. Well, long story short—"

"No. No long story short. I want to hear it step by step. Unless you're in a hurry."

He grinned. "Not me. So—here goes. First in this chain was how Phyllis's observations matched Ms. Piffle's, which led her to identify Bulldog. From there, we found the bar where he and Keziah met. Getting her recent picture spurred me on. I had a hunch she might have met other men there."

"Other men. Namely Franklin."

"Namely Franklin. I was too geared up to wait another day. But I did check with Will before heading out to Rowdy's with the new photo. I had even better luck than I expected. Mike Palacio, the bartender, recognized Keziah right away and called over one of the regulars to look at the picture.

"This guy recognized her too. He happened to be outside when this big brawl broke out in the parking lot. According to him, Keziah and her date—presumably Franklin—were walking across the lot, arm in arm, when this 'wild woman' literally jumped on them and started beating the, uh, tar out of them. As soon as he could get away, Franklin ran in the opposite direction. Apparently Keziah was in no condition to fight back, and the woman dragged her into her car."

"Why didn't this—witness—report it?"

"He did tell Mike—after it was all over. Mike checked outside and didn't see any sign of anything wrong, so he decided the guy was just exaggerating. I asked the witness the same question today, and he said it wasn't up to him to 'interfere in family disputes.'"

"So he knew it was 'family'—Keziah's mother."

"Yeah. I left out the screaming part. Mrs. Porter had a lot to say to Keziah. A lot of it starting with 'No daughter of mine.'"

"Is that how Jemma fit in? No daughter of hers?"

"Indirectly. I suspected the guy had too much to drink that night and would back off if he thought my questions might go in that direction. So I buttered him up and told him how helpful he'd been, which was true. Then I asked if he could tell me anything else Mrs. P. had said. As best he could remember, she said something like, 'Your sister's a...blankety-blank whore too, and I'll make her pay. When the time comes.'"

"What made you think the time was now?"

"Partly because I'd just learned about the way Mrs. P. acted in the parking lot. But mostly, I thought about her breaking into Jemma's place in broad daylight, and I realized she was getting bolder—and even more erratic. I didn't know *when* she'd strike, but—I was convinced she would. Sometime. And I didn't want to take any chances.

"I'd have gone over to Jemma's right away myself, but I had a call across town I had to take care of. So I phoned Elise. It didn't take much to persuade her to check on Jemma ASAP. I didn't know you were still there."

"I never could have handled the situation by myself."

"Don't discount your part. If you hadn't been there, no telling what that crazy woman would have done. Her plan, whatever it was, got derailed."

"Sharon, I could never have handled the situation by *myself*."

Startled, I looked up to see Elise, who'd just come into the room. We'd been so caught up in Tom's story, she'd slipped in unnoticed.

CHAPTER 52

"I'm not going to get us bogged down in 'what ifs,'" Elise continued. "But I'm thankful you were there to 'derail' her, as Tom says."

"How is Jemma now?"

"They're keeping an eye on her, but Dr. McConaghy thinks she can go home shortly. She's coping as best she can, and I need to get back to her soon. But I wanted to join you all for a few minutes."

As if hearing his name caused a Pavlovian response, Dr. McConaghy appeared to report on Jemma's condition. "There's shock, and then there's shock. Doctor-speak. Fortunately, she responded before shutting down. Physically, she's strong and resilient. Psychologically—well, time will tell. But she couldn't have a better nurse than Elise." His eyes twinkled. "I keep trying to lure her away from Dr. Taitte."

Elise smiled at Dr. McConaghy. "I'm glad you were the doctor on call."

He chuckled. "Evading the bait as usual." He gave us all a wave and continued on his rounds.

Elise looked at me in her usual compassionate way. "Something else I'm grateful for, Sharon. Jemma hasn't said much about what went on back there. She might have blocked it out of her mind, and I don't think now is a good time to bring it up.

"But she did make a couple of oddly connected statements. She told me you agreed with me that she was nothing like her mother and that her mother's brain disease was caused by a car accident. What disease? What accident? She'd told me her father was paralyzed in an accident, but she never mentioned that her mother was involved too."

"The disease is just a guess—a likely guess, I hope. The accident was so long ago—I think she was only about five or six years old—and her father's condition was so traumatic, and obvious, it probably never occurred to her that her mother was affected too. I guess physically the woman was unscathed. It wasn't till Jemma and I got to talking about it that she realized there were other signs a five-year-old wouldn't have noticed."

"That makes perfect sense. I'm sure they're doing a CT scan on Mrs. Porter." Elise put her hand over her heart. "No, I didn't kill her, thank God. At first, I was afraid I hadn't hit her hard *enough*, but when she didn't come to right away...."

Elise regained her composure. "They'll probably keep her overnight. I'll check on her prognosis. Or maybe I won't. We'll just leave it that she's brain-injured."

"Whatever the results of her medical tests," Tom said with grim satisfaction, "she's facing a nice little arrest warrant."

Not so nice or so little, I suspected, stifling a cheer. Her troubles with CYFD would be minuscule in comparison to what lay ahead.

Elise looked at her watch, then turned to me. "I need to go soon. But before I do, can you tell me what caused Jemma to go into near-shock? All Tom said when he called was that Mrs. Porter had gone berserk and Jemma was in danger."

"I can explain in more detail later if you'd like. For now, the most crucial thing, the thing that sent Jemma over the edge...their mother is the one who killed Keziah."

Elise's fair skin turned even more ashen. "I never guessed she would cross that line. But I suppose I shouldn't be surprised."

"Poor Jemma. As horrid as her mother is, Jemma simply couldn't cope with the fact that she'd do something so—so unimaginable."

"Another measure of Jemma's sanity." Elise's eyes blurred with unshed tears. "And something else—Jemma would never admit it openly, but I could tell from occasional remarks she made, deep down she had this unrealistic hope that her mother would undergo some kind of transformation. That she'd turn out to be someone other than who she is."

She is who she is. Something to ponder.

"What about Mr. Porter?" Ryan asked. "Up there alone. Can he manage by himself?"

"Omigosh!" Elise said. "I'll get in touch with social services right away! If worse comes to worst, he can always go into a nursing home."

"Don't worry about that," Tom said. "Someone is up at their place right now with a search warrant. That area will be cordoned off, and Mr. Porter will be moved someplace safe. Technically, he's an accessory, but in his condition, well, who knows."

"Maybe I'm being unrealistic too," I said, "but I like to think he didn't go along with his wife—that he simply didn't have any way to stop her."

"You're probably right," Elise said. "Jemma was hurt that he abandoned them emotionally. But maybe he saw himself as much a victim as the girls. Lots of hostility to sort through. Too much to think about now. Right now I'm going to look in on Jemma."

CHAPTER 53

Wednesday—our last day here. Time to pack our bags and say our goodbyes.

Although it was only mid-morning when we arrived at Jemma's, we were greeted by brightly lit, colorful twinkle lights adorning her house.

"We planned the same surprise for each other," Jemma said as she ushered us inside, "but Elise beat me to it. It was a wonderful homecoming!"

"Thanks to Tom," Elise said. "I enlisted his help to welcome us home. He hung the lights and brought the picture back while we were gone."

Another cheerful surprise was seeing the picture of Jemma and Keziah hanging on the wall across from us. A reminder of sweeter times.

"I'm still not ready to talk about—anything—just yet. But I'm healing," Jemma told us.

"That she is," Elise said, and the smile that passed between them told me Jemma was truly on the mend, despite the rough road they faced.

Elise invited us into the kitchen, where she had just taken a batch of bizcochitos out of the oven. Ryan especially enjoyed the treat since he'd missed out on the gingerbread the day before.

"I hope you doubled the recipe," he said as he helped himself to his sixth cookie.

Elise laughed. "I tripled the recipe, so I'll have a goodie bag for you to take home with you. Everyone has to have bizcochitos for Christmas."

I groaned. "At the rate we're gobbling these down, it might take a crane to get us to the airport."

We promised to keep in touch, then made the same promises to Tom and Will and—later—to our friends at the Teen Center.

"Any last advice, partner?" Tom asked me.

Yeah. Ditch Rowena. "No, not really. Give my regards to Cindy. I hope...." *I hope she and Jemma make amends.* I wasn't sure how much Tom knew about their rift, so decided that was better left unsaid too.

"You hope she dumps Roque?"

"Heavens, no. I barely remember him. What I meant was—I hope she'll drop by to see Jemma."

"I know they were kind of on the outs," he admitted. "But Cindy did send her flowers. So that's a good sign."

"Speaking of advice, any last words for us?"

"I wish you'd both move up here. Till then, practice your parallel turns, Sharon. Next time you can do black diamonds with Ryan and me."

Ryan grinned. "Right. We'll both slalom down our driveway. Hone our skills."

"Sounds like I'd better keep in practice too." Tom hesitated a beat. "Before you go, Sharon, there is something I probably ought to let you know.... You asked me what made me think Jemma was in danger. Your hunch was something I factored in."

"My hunch? I didn't know I had a hunch."

"Well, your intuition. Whatever you want to call it. You felt uneasy without knowing why. By itself, it wasn't something I'd act on. But added to the things that triggered the alarm—the incident at Rowdy's plus the break-in at Jemma's—it carried some weight."

"Thanks for telling me. Maybe I'll pay more attention to my intuition from now on instead of always trying to find logical reasons for everything."

* * *

Wilma glared at me over her glasses. "You're not just saying that, are you? About keeping in touch?"

I lifted her chin with my fingers and looked her in the eye. "No. With me, a promise is a promise."

She looked pleased, though she didn't actually smile.

"I'm going to bring up my grades," Dot said. "You made another promise, remember? About a recommendation letter?"

I laughed. "I remember that one too. But I certainly hope I see you before then. We'll be back again. That's another promise."

Brenda smiled. She and I had discussed that promise, but I wanted it to be a surprise to the girls.

Phyllis threw her arms around me. "I'll miss you."

"Me too you. All of you. You all be good to each other."

Dot gave me a heartfelt hug, Wilma a shy one.

In appreciation for his help in the shop, one of the kids had created a hand-tooled belt for Ryan—and all the shop kids had signed a thank-you card for him.

"Don't get mushy now, Mr. S," one of the boys called out.

"Aw, shucks—just what I'd planned to do."

Everyone laughed, and I was able to keep my own mushiness at bay.

* * *

Back at The Lodge, I phoned Cat.

"Tell me everything!" she said.

"All in good time, m'dear. First things first. Brenda and Darryl invited us back next month to see the production of *Oklahoma!* The kids took up a collection for all four of us. I think there's enough to buy us a meal or two."

"Oh, Sharon. Why not? All Steve and I have talked about is how we'd love to go back and do nothing but *enjoy* ourselves this time."

"Let's make that a promise!" *What's one more promise among friends?*

CHAPTER 54

"Hi, Mom. I've been thinking about you."

"Oh, hello, Sharon dear. I'm glad you called. I was thinking about you too."

"You were?"

"Yes. I just found out something I thought you'd be interested in. Your Great-Great-Uncle Gunnar was a lawyer too."

"That's nice. What kind of law did he practice?"

"I don't know. Does it matter?"

"No. Just curious."

"He's a descendant of Knut the Valiant, which means we're related too. Knut's great-grandfather...."

I looked at my watch and began to time her monologue. That familiar vise-like sensation began gripping me, crushing the breath out of me. Then I let it go.

When she finally started winding down, I cleared my throat and said, "Mom, you are who you are, and that's okay."

"What are you talking about, Sharon? Sometimes you don't make any sense at all."

"I know. I am who I am. Well, Mom, it's been nice chatting with you, but I gotta run now."

I closed the phone slowly and inhaled deeply, feeling both sad and oddly at peace. I sat quietly for a few moments longer, staring at nothing in particular.

Then on impulse I called Ryan's mom.

"Mijita! I'm so glad to hear from you!"

Somehow, I could feel the exclamation points; I could feel the warmth in her voice across hundreds of miles of cell-phone airwaves. And I felt desperately homesick.

"I miss you," was all I could think to say.

"We miss you too! Tell me all about your trip!"

"Oh my, it would take too long to tell in a phone call. But we'll be back soon—in plenty of time for Christmas—and you'll get an earful, I promise."

"We'll have a big family barbacoa! Well, maybe just a little family one."

I closed my eyes and smiled. Even a little family event in the Salazar household means lots of people. "Good."

"Alana and I have been waiting to make tamales till you're here to help. It wouldn't be the same without you! And besides that, I'll make those chalupas you like so much!"

"I love you, Amá.

"I love you también, mijita! Come home soon!"

I will.

CPSIA information can be obtained at www.ICGtesting.com
Printed in the USA
BVOW011144111112

305236BV00001B/18/P